Dear Reader

Inspiration for the novels I write sometimes emerges from the unlikeliest of places. The idea for the story of Sophie and Will's bumpy journey along the road to finding love originated from a TV documentary about a rundown inner-city suburb destined for destruction. It was saved by a courageous and spirited group of people, determined to make better lives for themselves.

To outsiders, the residents of my fictional suburb of Prevely Springs have little hope of ever achieving that elusive *better life*. Will Brent—an overworked, brooding but devoted GP—tries his best to help, but it takes the addition of a bubbly socialite from the other side of the country, with a mission to *make a difference*, Dr Sophie Carmichael, to turn his hopes and dreams into reality and release him from his tortured past.

I wanted to show a community working together to overcome serious and sensitive problems as a backdrop to the unlikely romance between my hero and heroine, and their attempt to overcome their own inner demons. I believe the more difficult the journey, the greater the satisfaction at arriving at the final destination.

I hope you enjoy reading my story about Sophie, Will and the people of Prevely Springs as much as I enjoyed writing it.

Leonie

Originally a city girl, **Leonie Knight** grew up in Perth, Western Australia. Several years ago, with her husband, two young sons and their Golden Retriever, she moved south to a small rural acreage located midway between dazzling white beaches and the magnificent jarrah forest of the Darling Scarp. Now her boys have grown and left home, and the demands of her day-job have lessened, she finds she has more time to devote to the things she loves—gardening, walking, cycling, reading, and of course writing. She has spent most of her adult life working in first a suburban and then a rural general medical practice—combining that with the inspiration she gets from her real-life hero, it is only natural that the stories she writes are Medical™ Romances.

This is Leonie Knight's debut book!

SUDDENLY
SINGLE SOPHIE

BY
LEONIE KNIGHT

First published in Great Britain 2011
by Mills & Boon, an imprint of Harlequin (UK) Limited,
Eton House, 18-24 Paradise Road, Richmond, Surrey TW9 1SR

© Leonie Knight 2011

ISBN: 978 0 263 21908 1

Harlequin (UK) policy is to use papers that are natural, renewable
and recyclable products and made from wood grown in sustainable
forests. The logging and manufacturing processes conform to the
legal environmental regulations of the country of origin.

Printed and bound in Great Britain
by CPI Antony Rowe, Chippenham, Wiltshire

SUDDENLY
SINGLE SOPHIE

To my unfailingly supportive husband, Colin,
and my amazing writing friends,
Anna, Teena, Lorraine, Susy and Claire.
Thank you for your faith in me.

PROLOGUE

'YOU'RE better off without him.'

Sophie Carmichael's body-racking sobs began to subside as her best friend Anna put her arm around her shoulder and gave it a reassuring squeeze. Sophie reached for a handful of tissues and noisily blew her nose. Venting her distress in a tearful outburst definitely helped ease the rawness she felt. She took a deep breath and managed a wilted smile.

'I still can't understand how he could be so cold...and two-faced,' Sophie said. 'He didn't even have the courage to tell me to my face.'

'It could have been worse. He might have broken up with you with a text message. Vanessa's boyfriend—'

'I know, I heard. But they'd only been together for two minutes, not nearly two years.' Sophie wiped away the last of her tears and felt her fighting spirit begin to return. It made sense now why Jeremy had stopped pleading with her to move in with him. He apparently wanted a live-in lover, not a wife. And he'd found one—who was now pregnant with his child. She'd wondered if the two of them had planned the whole scenario.

Sophie clenched her teeth, not wanting to believe her ex was capable of such blatant and calculated cheating. She wasn't going to let a two-timing, deceitful rat like her ex-fiancé ruin her life, though.

'Didn't Jeremy make it quite clear he didn't want kids until he'd finished his training and set up in private practice?'

'That's right. And muggins me went along with it.' Sophie slumped back in her seat and sighed. She tried to stand back from her churning emotions and look at the situation objectively. 'You're right, you know. I'm glad I found out about Jeremy's unfaithfulness before we actually tied the knot. I *am* better off without him.'

The women sat in silent contemplation for a minute or two before Anna finally spoke.

'What are you going to do now?'

Sophie had asked herself that same question a hundred times over the past weeks since she'd found out about Jeremy's infidelity by overhearing a conversation at the hospital where he worked. She had naively believed it was purely unfounded gossip. When she'd confronted him, though, he'd not wasted words in telling her the brutal truth. It seemed everyone had known before she had. She'd never felt so humiliated in her life and was grateful the news hadn't spread to the staff of her father's general practice where she worked.

At least she'd been able to choose the time and place to tell her parents—but it hadn't made it any easier. Her father's attitude had left her firstly stunned and then outraged. Ross Carmichael still thought the sun shone from Jeremy's nostrils and seemed to believe they'd get back together again. She couldn't believe he could be so insensitive to *her* feelings. Her mother had hardly disguised her disappointment. She'd often reminded Sophie of her relentlessly ticking biological clock and didn't like the idea of the mob of grandchildren she so dearly wanted being put on hold. Of course Sophie still wanted a family but now, at thirty-one, unceremoniously dumped and unexpectedly single, she was in no hurry.

'I really don't know. I haven't had a chance to think about it but one thing I do know for sure.'

'And what's that?' Anna was stroking Sophie's cat, which had jumped up on her lap, probably sensing the calmer of the two women was Anna.

'I'm going to steer clear of men for a while.'

Anna smiled. 'They're not all rotten, you know.'

'I didn't say they were, but—'

'You need a break. I can understand that. It's early days.'

Max, Sophie's Burmese bundle of masculine feline charm, gracefully stretched, began purring loudly and rubbed his chin on Anna's thigh, as if defending the male of the species.

'Maybe you need a holiday,' Anna continued.

'A permanent holiday.' Sophie suddenly realised what she really needed was a working holiday; a complete break from her predictable life. She'd always had her father, or Jeremy, or the expectations of the high-flying social set she moved in to make the big life decisions for her. Or at least nudge her in a certain direction. It hadn't bothered her in the past, but now... She felt manipulated, controlled and wanted a taste of freedom. If she made mistakes, at least they would be her own.

'I might look at leaving Sydney for a while, maybe head north.' She paused and felt her heart pumping faster. It was a lightbulb moment and made a great deal of sense. She would only stagnate in her father's practice and was tired of listening to the woes of the affluent, worried well-to-do. She remembered when, as an enthusiastic new graduate, she'd wanted her work to make a real difference to her patients' lives. There was little chance of that happening if she stayed where she was. Her mind started to work in overdrive.

'Or even west. I've heard there's a shortage of GPs over in Perth.'

Anna looked only mildly surprised, as if she'd been expecting it.

'Well, good for you, Dr Sophie.' She lifted Max from her lap and dumped the protesting cat on the floor then added, 'How about we open that bottle of wine I brought?'

'Great idea. And I'll see if I can rustle up some comfort food,' Sophie said with a grin. She felt renewed, ready to take on whatever challenges life presented.

While Anna uncorked the Chardonnay, Sophie loaded generous serves of chocolate cheesecake on plates.

When they sat down again, Anna raised her glass.

'To your new life,' she said as they clinked glasses.

'Without the complication of men,' Sophie added.

CHAPTER ONE

'SHE'S here. Come and have a look,' Caitlyn called from the tea room.

Dr William Brent didn't share his young receptionist's excitement at what he presumed was the arrival of the new doctor. It was barely twenty minutes since the last patient had left. Saturday morning clinics were supposed to finish at midday and today he'd particularly wanted to run to schedule. But it was already after two o'clock, the time he'd planned to meet Dr Sophie Carmichael.

She was late. Not an ideal start.

He was a busy man and didn't have spare time to waste on waiting. He had a house call after the interview and a meeting with a builder scheduled for mid-afternoon.

He dismissed his annoyance in the name of an urgent need for an assistant and hoped Caitlyn was right.

Sophie Carmichael's phone call, just over a month ago, had come at the right time and he'd invested a considerable amount of energy in getting the well-qualified Sydney doctor to relocate, even if it turned out to be for only a couple of months.

'Quick, you've got to see this, Dr Brent.' Caitlyn stood in the doorway to his office with a broad grin on her face and Will couldn't help but feel a sense of foreboding.

Why was Caitlyn so excited and, worse, why was she grinning?

He followed her down the short corridor to the tea room and peered through the small, grubby window.

'Oh, my God!' The words escaped before Will had time to check them and now he understood why his young receptionist was so insistent he have an advanced viewing.

Will glanced at Caitlyn, who was still grinning, but couldn't stop his eyes returning to the new arrival. His heart dropped. She was driving a nippy little sports car. He didn't usually trust first impressions but had the gut feeling this stern-faced young woman, whom he could see clearly in the open-topped vehicle, would be as at home in his practice as caviar at a sausage sizzle.

But he was truly desperate.

Working twelve-hour days, being on call weekends and after hours, as well as trying to find time to get his plans for the community centre off the ground was wearing him down to near breaking point. There just weren't enough hours in the day.

He had to keep an open mind.

'If that's the new doc, I hope she's better at fixing sick people than she is at parking her car,' Caitlyn said.

Will squinted through the dirty glass, watching the wine-red cabriolet being manoeuvred into a space that was way too small.

'Ouch.' He felt the scrape of metal on metal as the front-end passenger side didn't quite clear the carport post. If she was the new doctor, and Will had no reason to think otherwise, it was definitely not a good start to their working relationship.

But the show wasn't over.

The woman seemed to be having problems unfolding the roof to secure the vehicle. She huddled over the dash and first the windscreen wipers activated then the hazard lights flashed before the roof finally jerked into place. She abandoned the car and squeezed her petite frame into the gap between her fancy sports car and Will's elderly, slightly battered station wagon. She was in shadow so Will could no longer see her face, but her body language clearly conveyed frustration and anger. He was fascinated. Mesmerised, even.

'Look what she's wearing.' Caitlyn was obviously enjoying the spectacle but her tip-off was unnecessary. How could anyone *not* notice the woman's outfit? It was so out of place for a meeting, no matter how informal, with her new employer. She wouldn't last five minutes in this neighbourhood decked out in low-slung, skin-tight black jeans with lolly-pink high-heeled sandals and a top that was body-hugging, and exposing more skin than…

'Whoops. She's seen us.' The girl's attempt to duck away from the window wasn't quick enough, but at least she'd tried to look discreet. Will suddenly realised his jaw was gaping and he snapped his mouth shut the moment the woman's blazing eyes met his. But he couldn't take his eyes off her. He could see her more clearly now and there was something about the determined thrust of her jaw and the resolute expression on her fine-featured face that captivated him.

It didn't take her long to compose herself, though. She smiled and waved as she hoisted a large bag over her shoulder and headed towards the back staff entrance.

'I'll put the kettle on, then?' At least Caitlyn was thinking sensibly. He needed a coffee.

'Good idea. I'll go and meet her.'

He took a couple of deep breaths, ran his fingers through his too-long hair and smiled as he opened the back door.

Sophie Carmichael had finally arrived at the Prevely Springs Medical Clinic. She was tired, frustrated and wondering if she'd made a huge mistake. Not sleeping the previous night, coupled with an inconvenient run of bad luck, hadn't helped. She felt like getting on the first flight back to Sydney.

The move to Western Australia was supposed to be about taking control of her life but obstacles had appeared at every turn. She should have arrived in Perth in plenty of time to make it to the hotel she'd booked for the night. She'd planned to at least get a few hours' sleep and then shower and change before her interview.

But the best-laid plans…

Firstly her plane had been delayed and she'd been forced to sit in the airport lounge for most of the night. Then, on her arrival in Perth, she'd discovered her luggage had been lost. Now she was fifteen minutes late for her meeting with her future employer because the airport taxi driver had taken her to the wrong rail depot to pick up her car…the beautiful, brand-new sports car she'd bought only a week ago as a symbol of her new-found freedom. Which now had an ugly gouge down one side due to a momentary lapse of concentration.

She tried to focus on the positives.

She'd never been a quitter.

Leaving home hadn't been a mistake.

She wasn't running away from her problems, just taking a break to regroup.

Her objective while in Perth was to work, and learn, and prove to herself she wasn't afraid of leaping out of her comfort zone into the wild unknown.

She also planned to show her toad of a fiancé that she was quite capable of fulfilment…and independence…and happiness… without him.

She scowled.

Jeremy…her fiancé… Not any more.

It hadn't taken as much courage as she'd thought to relocate to the other side of the country, even if it was only for a couple of months. The last thing she needed was a holiday with endless empty time on her hands—work was definitely the answer, and work on the other side of the country was perfect. She needed time out without having to deal with the tattered remnants of her life; without the distraction of the opposite sex; without having to get approval for everything she did from her father or Jeremy.

'Things can't possibly get any worse,' she muttered as she locked the car. She glanced at the single visible window and caught a glimpse of two curious faces not quite pressed against the glass. One was a teenage girl and the other…

She instantly forgot her troubles.

The dark-haired man was half smiling, and even through the grubby glass she could see he was…absolutely gorgeous.

He waved and then ducked away from the window as if he'd been caught in the act of being nosy.

Then he reappeared.

When she saw him standing in the doorway, all mussed-up hair, baggy clothes and brooding dark, black-brown eyes, she *knew* she'd made the right decision in leaving Sydney.

If this man was Dr Brent, it would be no hardship to work with him but she'd have to be careful. He was too damned attractive for his own good and she'd bet her last dollar he had no idea he had all the attributes to turn women's heads.

Slinging her bag on her shoulder, she strode towards the ramp leading up to the back entrance. She still couldn't rationalise the preconceived image she'd conjured up of Dr Brent, with the man standing in the doorway.

On the phone he'd come across as kind, conservative, passionate about his job and desperate for a second GP to share his increasing patient load. He'd also sounded…weary.

She'd thought he'd be middle-aged and suspected he might be looking for someone young and fresh to share the patient load at the practice, if the wording in his ad in the widely read *Australian General Practice* magazine was anything to go by. He'd really wanted someone who was prepared to commit long term, with a view to partnership.

But it appeared that type of candidate was thin on the ground and she definitely wasn't that person either. She had no illusions that her escape from her failed relationship and the gossip of Sydney's heartless, egocentric socialites was anything but temporary. She just needed time to heal.

Sophie was totally realistic about her future. She had solid reasons to return to the city she loved. All her friends were in

Sydney; she owned a beachside apartment at Collaroy she didn't want to give up; and had adopted a feisty feline named Max that she couldn't leave in her friend Anna's care for ever. She planned to go home as soon as the fallout from her broken relationship settled, and she'd made sure Dr Brent knew she wasn't planning on staying permanently.

And the reality of this man standing in the doorway had just made her decision to have a break much easier.

Could this seriously good-looking hunk possibly be her new boss?

She was about to find out.

For a moment Will Brent was spellbound by the woman's penetrating china-blue eyes, fascinated by the tilt of her cute, lightly freckled nose, captivated by her hesitant smile.

'I'm Will Brent and I assume you're Dr Carmichael. Can I take your bag?' he asked as he extended his hand in greeting.

She offered hers and it felt cool, soft and damp. Was she nervous?

'Yes. Please, call me Sophie, and, no, thanks. I'll be fine.'

'Come in,' he said in what he hoped was a welcoming tone.

She repositioned the bag on her shoulder as she stepped from the short ramp into the building. He suspected she could be just what the practice needed. So if her first impression of Prevely Springs Medical Clinic was to go as smoothly as he'd planned, he'd have to remain totally objective, professional...look beyond the attractively packaged woman standing on his threshold.

Attractive didn't mean dependable. It meant the pain of betrayal; it meant shallow; it meant priorities very different from his. What twisted lapse of judgement had let him fall in love all those years ago?

Will did a quick reality check.

He had no right to prejudge or compare.

Sophie Carmichael was simply a colleague, who happened to be beautiful.

And he mustn't think of her in any other way.

There was no way he could burden *any* woman with his problems. He still felt the hurt and disappointment of his past and the weight of the emotional debt he was struggling to pay. He had *chosen* to lead a solitary life in the rough inner-city suburb he'd grown up in. And he'd made a promise, nearly twenty years ago, to stay and in some way give back to this community.

Love, marriage, children… The fantasy just didn't fit with the dark reality of his life.

He'd caused the two people he'd loved most in the world so much anguish. There wasn't a day went by when his heart didn't fill with regret for those angry, irresponsible teenage years that had shaped his future. His devotion to his practice and the salt-of-the-earth people in the Springs was the only way he knew to repay his grandparents, and he often lamented that they weren't alive to witness his achievements.

He'd only recently admitted, though, that he needed help to keep going. The long hours he worked, being on call weekends and after hours, was wearing him down to near breaking point. He had high hopes for the woman standing in front of him.

Releasing Sophie's fingers from his grip, he did a lightning rethink of where he could conduct the interview but came to the conclusion every room in the building was in a similar state of disarray to his own.

Better the mess you know…

Usually it wouldn't bother him but he felt an unsettling compulsion to make a good impression and wished he'd chosen something more stylish to wear than his crumpled khaki chinos and faded short-sleeved checked shirt. But she'd find out soon enough that tidiness and fashion weren't high on his priority list.

He cleared his throat in an attempt to take his mind off Sophie Carmichael's creamy smooth shoulders and the soft curve of her neck. Somehow the inappropriateness of her attire didn't seem so important any more.

'We'll go down to my consulting room. It's the second door on the right,' Will said in a voice he hardly recognised.

She followed him down to his room and he stepped back to let her in first. Glancing around the cluttered office, he wondered if the hint of a frown on her face was due to disapproval. She was probably used to working in much more luxurious surroundings and he hoped she wouldn't be put off.

'Please, sit down.'

She sat in one of the patient chairs, legs crossed, hands resting in her lap, and he wondered what she was thinking. He'd done his best to prepare her.

The couple of times he'd talked to her on the phone he'd been totally honest with her, revealing Prevely Springs was an underprivileged area. But he'd told her the work was challenging and potentially rewarding. To her credit, she'd still seemed keen. Her agreement to commit to even a few weeks with him had rekindled a light at the end of what had recently become a very long, dark tunnel.

He didn't want her to change her mind.

'I've been looking forward to meeting you. Your CV was impressive, your references excellent.' He sent her what he hoped was an encouraging smile.

'Thanks,' she said.

Her credentials were almost too good to be true. But the phone conversation he'd had with her two days ago had allayed his concerns that the inevitable culture shock would be an obstacle for her.

She cleared her throat and Will wondered if the colour in her previously pale cheeks was a reaction to his praise.

'I...er...' She looked away as if composing her thoughts. *Was* she having second thoughts?

He knew she had a privileged background. She'd been educated at one of the most expensive ladies' colleges and graduated from medical school with top marks. He suspected her life choices had been easy and uncomplicated. He *had* wondered at her motivation in wanting to work in a practice so different to what she was used to.

She came from a medical family. Her father was a well-known and highly regarded GP in Sydney and Sophie had worked in his practice for the past two years. It had surprised Will that Dr Ross Carmichael had telephoned him a week ago and, in a roundabout way, had seemed to be checking *his* credentials. Will, in fact, had been annoyed at some of his questions and the cross-examination had struck him as being a little beyond normal protective paternal behaviour. Sophie seemed like someone who could look after herself quite capably.

He dragged his mind back to the task in hand. Sophie looked uncomfortable.

'I, um, owe you an apology.'

Now, that was something he hadn't expected.

A lock of Sophie's thick red-brown hair escaped from the clasp holding it in place, and as she tucked it behind her ear Will noticed an almost imperceptible tremor in her fingers

'An apology?'

She folded her arms across her chest.

'You must be wondering why I'm dressed like this.'

Yes, of course he was, but he didn't want to draw attention to her relaxed dress code. Well, not until he'd confirmed her commitment.

'I take it you're planning to wear something a little more conservative…' *less provocative* was another description that came to mind '…to work.'

Rosy colour swept into her neck and flooded her face.

'I'm sorry,' Will said, although he wasn't quite sure what he'd done to make her blush.

She took a deep breath.

'My plane was delayed so I didn't get here until this morning. Then it took another hour and a half for the airline to verify that my luggage had been mislaid. And the taxi driver who drove me to Wellesley to collect my car hardly spoke a word of English. So even if I'd had time to change—'

He'd heard enough, and doubted she could fabricate such an elaborate combination of misadventures. He understood why she had faint dark shadows under her eyes. She most likely needed rest rather than a grilling from him.

'Ah...I see. You've not had the best introduction to the west. You must be exhausted.' He thought of a dozen questions he wanted to ask but they would just have to wait. After all, he'd told her on the phone the job was hers and all he needed to do was discuss her duties, finalise her hours and sort out the paperwork.

'The interview is a formality, really. It's basically so we can introduce ourselves. You can ask me any questions about the work, the practice, anything you'd like to know, before you start next week.'

She leaned towards him, interlocked her fingers and placed her hands on his desk. The pose struck him as being assertive without being arrogant. Her anxiety seemed to have vanished.

Maybe she would be okay dealing with some of the rougher elements that were inevitably part of his practice.

'I'm looking forward to it,' she said. 'I haven't got any questions.'

'Great.' The interview was going well but there was one more thing he had to discuss and he didn't want to put pressure on her. 'We haven't talked about how long you're prepared to work here. I realise you're not planning on staying long term, but even a few weeks will be a great help to me.' He thought of the long-lost luxury of spare time. 'Does a period of six to eight weeks sound agreeable?' That would let him at least get the ball rolling with a time-consuming task he wasn't looking forward to—organising fundraising for the community centre. 'With the option of staying longer, of course.' He sent her what he hoped was a charismatic smile.

'That would suit me fine,' she said with a look that suggested relief.

At that moment Caitlyn appeared, cheerful as ever, with two steaming cups and a plate of biscuits.

'Thanks, Caitlyn.'

'That's okay, Dr Brent.' The girl cleared a space on Will's desk by pushing a jumble of referral pads to one side. She set down the cups.

'No problem. Have a good weekend.' She paused. 'Oh, and you told me to remind you about the home visit to Mrs Farris.'

'Thanks, I hadn't forgotten. See you next week.'

Six weeks was perfect, Sophie thought as she reached for one of the mugs filled with coffee she now felt sufficiently relaxed to drink. It was long enough to make her father understand she wasn't going to run back home after a week or two. She also thought of Jeremy and reminded herself she wanted to get as far away from him and his new girlfriend as possible, at least until the gossip died down.

And then she thought of Will Brent. How easy it was to like and admire him. She suspected he was close to burn-out and hoped she could give him the break he deserved. She felt certain she could learn a lot from him.

'Would you like a biscuit?' Will Brent's voice snapped her out of her reverie, but before she had a chance to reply there was a loud thumping on the front door.

'Is anyone there?' A man's voice boomed loud and urgent. 'Doc Brent, I need a doctor quick!'

There was no doubt about the genuine distress he conveyed and Will was out of his seat in an instant. He grabbed a large bunch of keys from a desk drawer, glanced briefly at Sophie with an expression that invited her to follow and headed towards the front of the building.

Through the frosted glass panels of the door Sophie could

make out the dark shape of a man who appeared to be carrying a child.

Will opened the door and a stocky man wearing full football kit, including boots, stumbled in. A boy of about four or five, dressed in an almost identical outfit, lay limp and wheezing in his arms.

'Thank God you're still here.'

The child opened his eyes but barely had the energy to whimper as Will took him gently from the man Sophie assumed was his father.

'How long's he been like this, Steve?' Will voiced his first question with just the right mix of authority and empathy. He obviously knew the pair and was leading them past the reception desk into a well-equipped treatment room. He laid the child down, adjusted the examination couch so the boy was sitting and placed an oximeter on his finger.

'No more than fifteen minutes. Jake was with me mates at the oval, watching the game, and they called me off the field.' The man pulled down his son's sock to reveal an angry red swelling just above his ankle. Sophie could see similar, smaller lesions on his arms.

'Bee sting,' he added, as if that explained everything. 'We know he's allergic, but the worst he's had in the past has been a rash.' He took a sharp intake of breath. 'He's never been this bad. It came on real quick. He can hardly breathe. We were going to the hospital but I saw your car—'

Steve was close to tears and began hyperventilating.

The last thing they needed in a situation where the boy should command Will's full attention was to have to deal with the father's panic attack as well.

Sophie felt her own tension climbing. The child was barely conscious and his breathing was becoming more laboured as each second passed. Will appeared remarkably calm.

'Sit down, Steve,' Will said coolly but firmly. 'Jake's going to be fine but I need to check him over.' He glanced in Sophie's direction. 'Can you organise a paediatric mask with high-flow oxygen?' He pointed to an emergency trolley next to an oxygen cylinder. Everything—medications, procedure packs, resuscitation equipment—was all labelled clearly and easy to find. 'And draw up…' He paused for a moment, calculating the crucial dose of lifesaving medication based on the boy's estimated weight. 'Point two of adrenaline for intramuscular injection.'

'Do you want nebulised adrenaline as well?' Sophie asked, trying to think ahead. She'd rarely treated emergencies in her father's practice but remembered the protocol from her hospital work. 'And an IV set?' she added as she positioned the mask on Jake's pale little face.

Will nodded. He worked incredibly quickly but gave the impression he was taking one quiet step at a time. Sophie drew up the medication, double-checked the dose and handed it to Will, who jabbed the needle into the boy's upper thigh so rapidly he hardly had time to respond. She could feel the tension decreasing in the room at about the same rate as the dusky grey colour in Jake's swollen lips began to turn the lightest shade of pink.

Will looked at the small device that measured oxygen levels in the blood. 'Ninety-four per cent,' he said as he placed a stethoscope on the little boy's chest and then checked his airway. The wheezing eased a little, but the movement of the muscles in Jake's abdomen and neck suggested he still had to work hard to get air in and out. Fortunately the risk of his larynx closing over completely had passed.

Will inserted an IV line while Sophie set up the nebuliser and together they stabilised the five-year-old to the point where Will had time to talk to Steve. He pulled up a chair opposite him.

'Jake's over the worst, Steve, but he's not out of the woods yet. He needs monitoring in hospital and I'm going to call an ambulance. He also needs blood tests and will probably go home with an EpiPen, possibly an asthma puffer as well. Do you know what an EpiPen is?'

'Yeah, I think you told us about it the first time Jake was stung. It's the injection you keep with you all the time, isn't it?'

'That's right.'

'Do you want me to ring the ambulance?' Sophie offered.

'Thanks, the local number is on the wall above the phone,' Will said with a grateful smile. 'I'll put the kettle on.'

A short time later, while the adults sat drinking coffee, crisis over, waiting for the ambulance, Jake slowly and steadily improved. Sophie marvelled at how composed Will was as he chatted to Steve.

'Daddy,' Jake said suddenly in a clear, loud voice as he pulled off the mask and frowned. All eyes turned towards him.

'What's the matter?' Steve said, a look of panic returning to his face.

'That goal you kicked…just before three-quarter time.'

The adults exchanged glances and Steve smiled for the first time since he'd arrived.

'Yeah, what about it?'

'It was awesome.'

Steve grinned with obvious pride and Will chuckled.

'You think so?'

Jake took a couple of rapid breaths as he raised his hand for a high five with his father. 'The best.'

The ambulance arrived a few minutes later and after it had left with its two passengers, Will turned to Sophie.

'That was an impromptu example of general practice in Prevely Springs. Think you can handle it?'

Coping with the work wasn't a problem for Sophie. She was looking forward to the challenge. The predicament she faced was how she was going uphold her promise, the vow she'd confidently uttered when she and her best friend had made a toast to her new life…*without the complication of men.*

She had the feeling it wasn't going to be easy.

'I'll give it my best shot,' she said.

CHAPTER TWO

AFTER the ambulance left, Sophie experienced a satisfaction she hadn't felt since working in the emergency department as a raw, idealistic intern. She had no doubt in her mind that Will had, calmly, without fuss or wanting any praise, saved young Jake's life.

And she had been part of it.

'Do you deal with many emergencies?' she asked as she brought two mugs of fresh coffee into the treatment room where Will was tidying up.

He took one of the mugs and smiled.

'About one or two a week.'

'Across the full spectrum?'

Sophie perched herself on the examination couch and Will sat in the seat recently vacated by Jake's father.

'Pretty well. There's probably more than the norm of physical violence, drug overdoses, that kind of thing. The clinic operates a little like a country outpost, without the problem of distance and isolation. I do my best to stabilise patients who need hospital care before sending them on.'

Sophie thought of how different it was from her father's practice.

'Where I worked in Sydney, the patients are more likely to ring the ambulance first in life-threatening situations... To save time.'

Will's dark eyes clouded and he looked past Sophie into the distance before he refocused.

'A lot of my patients have had bad experiences with hospitals, and doctors who don't know them. And I don't blame the hospital staff making judgements on appearances. We all do it...'

The appraisal took only a second or two but Sophie felt Will's gaze flick from her high-heel-clad feet to the top of her tousled head, taking in everything in between. She suddenly became self-conscious about *her* appearance and the impression she'd made when he'd first seen her.

Before Sophie could think of a reply, Will had downed the last of his coffee and stood, stuffing his stethoscope into his pocket. He looked impatient to leave.

'I'll take you round to the flat. It's nothing flash but is clean, has the basics and is about twenty minutes' drive from here.'

Will's sudden change of subject didn't go unnoticed by Sophie, and she guessed her boss was just as tired as she was.

'Not in Prevely Springs?' She'd assumed she'd be staying closer to Will's clinic.

'No, Sabiston's the name of the suburb. I thought...' He hesitated.

'Yes? You thought?'

'It's a more...upmarket suburb than the Springs.'

More like what she was used to...

He smiled, a fleeting indication that he genuinely cared about her welfare, and it occurred to her how easily she could fall for this gentle, softly spoken, work-weary man. He was everything her cocky, self-absorbed ex wasn't.

No! Get a grip of yourself.

She hardly knew the man and it was way too soon. The painful sting of shame was still fresh in her memory and she didn't want to risk going through the indignity again.

'Don't worry, I'll manage,' Sophie said.

'I hope so.' He took his keys from his pocket. 'There's just one thing more, before we go to the flat.'

'Yes?'

'I need to make a quick house call. A woman with pancreatic cancer. I'm sure it won't take long. She only lives around the corner.'

Another surprise. Will did house calls…after hours…on top of what she calculated to be more than a sixty-hour working week.

'You'll like Bella Farris,' he added.

'And…well…the sooner I start, the harder it will be to chicken out.'

Sophie was determined to prove to her new employer she was prepared to tackle working in Prevely Springs head on.

Will knocked on the door of the tidiest townhouse in a shabby block of six and went straight inside without waiting for an answer. Sophie followed close behind, scanning the interior as she entered. The front door opened directly into a cramped living-dining area with a kitchen at the back. A boy of about thirteen or fourteen sat in front of a television screen connected to a games machine. He was overweight, pale, and his eyes didn't leave the screen. A couple of empty fast-food containers lay abandoned on the floor beside him.

'Hi, Brad. Is your mum upstairs in the bedroom?' Will's tone was cheerful and undemanding.

'Yeah.'

'How is she?'

'Same.' The boy's gaze left the screen, flicked to Will, hovered on Sophie for a second and then returned to the noisy, animated action on the screen. 'Aw, hell!' the boy added when some bloody tragedy terminated another of his virtual lives.

'Dr Carmichael and I will go up and see her, then.'

'Mmm.'

Sophie followed Will up the narrow concrete stairs, vestiges of mud-brown fibres the only indication they had once been carpeted.

'Bella, it's Will,' he called as he reached the dimly lit passage at the top of the stairs.

'In the bedroom.' The thin voice came from the only upstairs room with the door open. 'Come through.'

Sophie followed Will into a sparsely furnished room with a single small window overlooking a weedy back yard.

This family was struggling in more ways than one, Sophie thought as she smiled and nodded, acknowledging the woman propped up in a narrow bed near the window. Her spindle-like arms protruded from the bed cover and rested on her swollen abdomen. Her sighing breaths came irregularly.

'You've finally brought your girlfriend to meet me, have you, Dr Brent? About time too.' The woman smiled and a hint of colour advanced then rapidly retreated from Will's cheeks. She looked at Sophie and took a couple of deep breaths. Even talking appeared to be an effort for her. 'I told Will I wasn't going to leave this earth until he found a woman to replace me. He needs looking after.'

'Enough of your cheek, Bella.' Will put his medical bag down on the small table in a corner and sat on the end of her bed. 'This isn't my girlfriend. And you know that threat isn't going to work because you're not ready yet. Remember our little chat last week?'

He glanced over at Sophie, who was beginning to feel she was intruding in the relationship between these two people who were as close as a doctor and patient could be. Bella smiled with her eyes but her mouth remained in a grim line, suggesting she was in more pain than she let on.

'Who is she, then?'

'Dr Sophie Carmichael. She arrived this morning from Sydney to join the practice for a few weeks. Do you mind her sitting in?'

A look of disbelief flashed across Bella's face, as if the last thing she'd expected was for Sophie to be a doctor.

'Well, good for you, Sophie Carmichael.' She turned her head slightly to address Will. 'Of course I don't mind. Two heads are better than one.' She made a move to reposition herself on the pile of pillows behind her head, then grimaced and seemed to change her mind. 'You make sure you look after her and she might even stay more than a few weeks.' She turned to Sophie. 'Once you get to know him, he's not as bad as—'

'Enough, Bella. This isn't a social visit.'

Bella fixed her gaze back on Will and elevated an eyebrow. 'Of course not.'

'So what's been happening? How can I help?'

'Shelley insisted on calling you just to check. She thinks it's a blockage. I've not had a bowel movement for four days and I've got a new pain.' She pointed in the vague direction of her navel. 'And the nausea's a bit worse.'

Will got up and retrieved a file from the table where he'd left his bag and then returned to Bella's bedside. He looked across at Sophie. 'Shelley's one of the palliative care nurses.' He turned a couple of pages of the file Sophie assumed contained the nurse's notes. 'Your morphine dose has gone up in the last few days.'

'I vomited a couple of doses of the liquid yesterday and had to increase my night-time tablet.'

'What are you eating?'

'Not much.'

'How about fluids?' Will didn't labour the point.

'I'm keeping down a bit of water.'

Sophie admired Bella's uncomplaining courage, and as she watched Will examine his patient with large, gentle hands she felt admiration for him too.

'Well, what's the verdict?' Bella said when he'd finally finished. 'No beating around the bush.'

'I'm fairly sure the tumour is pressing on part of your intestine, causing a partial blockage.'

'What does that mean?'

'It means your food and drinks are passing through very slowly. It's probably why your pain and nausea are worse.'

'Oh.'

Sophie could see the stoic acceptance on Bella's face. She seemed to sense she didn't have long to live and trusted Will to do what he felt was best to make her last few weeks comfortable.

'I'll contact Shelley and ask her to organise for you to have your morphine by injection.' He went on to explain the device that would deliver a steady dose of the analgesic via a needle inserted into the fatty layer under the skin and a gadget called a syringe driver. It would overcome her problem of vomiting oral medication. 'One of the nurses reloads the medication daily. We can also mix in other drugs if needed, like an anti-emetic for nausea.'

Bella looked exhausted. 'Shelley said she'd come back this afternoon after you'd been.'

'Good. She can set up the pump. I'll also ask her to collect some dexamethasone from the pharmacy. If there's any swelling due to inflammation in the intestine, it should reduce it and might ease the blockage. It should help with the nausea too.'

'Okay. Best you two get on with enjoying the rest of your weekend.' Bella seemed to muster a last ounce of energy to wink and then she closed her eyes and sighed. 'Go on, then.'

Will and Sophie exchanged glances.

'I'll call in again Monday, Bella.'

The patient was breathing slowly. She appeared to be asleep, so the two doctors quietly left the room. Will made a quick phone call to Shelley before they went downstairs.

'Bye, Brad,' Sophie called as they let themselves out the front door.

The boy acknowledged their departure with a grunt and continued his game.

'How is Brad coping with his mother's illness?' Sophie asked as she buckled her seat belt in the passenger seat of Will's roomy old car.

'I don't think he is.' Will sighed and started the engine. 'I've tried to talk to him but he seems to have shut everyone out—including his mother. Bella worried about him at the beginning of her illness—she was diagnosed with cancer a week after Brad's fourteenth birthday—but she doesn't talk about him now. I think it upsets her that she can't give him the support she wishes she could. She told me a while back she'd run out of emotional energy.'

A painful mix of sadness and helplessness churned in Sophie's gut. The combination of poverty, illness and social isolation had delivered a cruel blow to this family. It wasn't fair.

'Isn't there anything more that can be done for Bella?'

'What do you mean?' Will frowned.

'She needs twenty-four-hour care… It's not fair on her son. There must be somewhere like a hospice… In Sydney—'

Will's grimace deepened.

'We're not in Sydney.'

Her boss seemed to want to wind up the conversation, but Sophie was determined to have her say.

'Isn't there residential care for the terminally ill here?'

Will began to back out into the street but braked at the kerb as a car sped past, the young driver going way too fast. He put the gearstick in neutral, wrenched the handbrake on and took a deep sighing breath.

'I wish there was…for patients like Bella.' Will's voice was thick with emotion. 'Do you think I don't know that Bella, and hundreds of people like her, deserve pampering and dignity in their last days? Or at least to have the choice of where and how they die. Particularly those who have little in the way of family support.' He paused. 'But who pays?'

Sophie looked away and began fiddling with her watch band.

'The government?' she suggested quietly.

Point made. Sophie felt foolish, naive and totally put in her place.

The hospice she was familiar with was a private facility attached to one of the major private hospitals, paid for by wealthy patients and their health insurance funds.

Will put the car in gear, released the handbrake and looked in the rear-view mirror but he didn't start reversing. He hadn't finished.

'The only government-funded hospice in this city is always full and is basically a converted wing of an old, now-defunct psychiatric hospital. And palliative care seems to be way down the list of priorities for Heath Department funding. I honestly think Bella is better off staying at home. At least for now.'

Will eased the car onto the road.

'She has access to twenty-four-hour advice, home visits through the palliative care service, and both she and Brad have chosen the home-care option.'

Will accelerated.

Sophie understood his frustration. She had a lot to learn—not only about working in Prevely Springs but about how much of himself he gave to his patients. She glanced at her companion. He had dark rings under his weary eyes and his tense grip on the steering-wheel indicated he wasn't as relaxed as his tone suggested.

What drove him to work so hard? As an experienced GP, surely he could choose a less demanding job. No one was indispensable.

But looking at Will... He seemed attached to his work and his patients by steadfastly unyielding Superglue.

Maybe she could be the one to ease his burden, to help him discover that there was a life away from work, to bring on that gorgeous smile she'd seen light up his face at least once that afternoon.

Purely as a friend, of course.

As if sensing Sophie was watching him, Will glanced at her as he slowed, approaching a corner.

'What's up?' he said, crinkling his brow in a frown.

Nothing that your amazing smile won't fix.

'I'm concerned about Brad.' Which she had been before she'd become distracted by the enigmatic man sitting next to her. She continued. 'What sort of life does he lead? What's in store for him in the future?' She paused to take a breath, aware she had Will's full attention. 'How can a fourteen-year-old shoulder the responsibility of being the primary carer for his mother? It should be the other way around.'

Will accelerated around the corner and Sophie recognised the street where the clinic was located. 'All valid concerns.' He sighed as if the weight of the whole world's problems rested on his shoulders. 'He seems to have shut the real world out and replaced it with a virtual one, I'm afraid. I'm at a loss as to how to help him.'

'Would it be okay with you if I tried to talk to Brad?' Sophie knew it was an impulsive offer, and any support she gave would be a drop in the ocean compared to the Farrises' hardship, but the boy seemed so isolated and withdrawn. She wanted to do something positive for Brad and Bella.

'You'd have nothing to lose because I've got little to offer him at the moment.' Will looked almost as weary as Bella. 'Maybe twelve or eighteen months down the track…'

His voice trailed off, as if he'd started a conversation he didn't want to finish, but Sophie was interested.

'What do you mean?'

'It's a long story.'

'I'm not in a hurry.'

He rewarded her with another of those charismatic smiles, apparently surprised she was interested.

'I'm in the process of trying to get a youth-focused community centre up and running.' Will parked on the road, a block away from the clinic. 'See, over there?'

Sophie looked in the direction he was pointing. On the far side of a sports field a building of about the same vintage as the clinic stood neglected at the end of a weedy driveway. Several windows were broken and the parts of a low front wall that weren't hidden by metre-high weeds were covered in graffiti. It had a chain-link fence around it, displaying a 'DANGER KEEP OUT' sign.

'Looks like it's ready for demolition.'

Will's scowl suggested he didn't agree.

'That's exactly what the council wants, but they haven't got the resources to replace it. Since they closed the place down about a year ago they took away the one place local kids, like Brad and his mates, could hang out without getting bored and up to mischief. But if it's up to bureaucracy, it's unlikely to happen.'

Will tapped his fingers on the steering-wheel and for the briefest moment he looked desolate. Why was finding the fate of a rundown old building so painful?

'So what's going to happen to it?'

'I'm trying to save it.'

'How?' Will was a man who seemed to have an insatiable need to take on projects that most people would discard into the too-hard basket. Surely he had enough to do, looking after the health needs of Prevely Springs, without taking on their social problems.

Will revved the engine and pulled out onto the road.

'The cost of renovating and refurbishing is much less than a new build, especially if the skills of local people could be utilised. I've submitted a plan to the council and...' His sigh suggested he wasn't overjoyed with their response. He focused his attention on traffic as he indicated to turn into the clinic.

'And...?'

He parked and turned off the engine.

'To cut a long story short, they wanted detailed plans and costing to present to the building committee and if they approve it goes to a general meeting. But—'

'Go on.'

'The wheels of local government turn slowly. It's unbelievably frustrating. Three months down the track, I'm still waiting for approval. But what's turning out to be a bigger problem is that the planning department tells me I'm going to have to show the community can raise funds for half the cost of renovating a very old building that the council think is only fit for demolition.'

'Before they give approval?'

'That's right.' The smile was gone and Will looked despondent.

'So it's not going to be a help for Brad and kids like him any time soon.'

'No.'

Will reached into the back to get Sophie's bag, a signal that the conversation was over. But Sophie wasn't about to be put off.

'How much?'

Will could no longer disguise his disillusionment.

'An impossible amount.'

'Nothing's impossible.' Sophie knew about fundraising for the sort of amounts that *would* be impossible if you depended on cake stalls and bring-and-buy sales. For some of her mother's friends, raising large amounts of money for charity was a very acceptable occupation.

'How much?'

'Two hundred thousand dollars.'

'Oh.'

'An awful lot of money.'

'Yes, I can understand the problem.'

But not impossible.

Sophie didn't want to labour the point when she had nothing tangible to offer. In Sydney in the same situation all she'd have to do would be to ask her parents to help. Her father would pull strings and know all the right people to ask for financial backing. And her mother revelled in organising high-profile events for charity. It helped that it was fashionable to donate to philanthropic worthy causes in certain circles.

But Prevely Springs was nothing like the eastern suburbs of Sydney. She doubted the community would even be considered *worthy*, let alone high profile enough to get the desired publicity that usually went with large donations.

Someone she hoped she could help, though, was Brad.

'Can I go with you on your next visit to Bella Farris and I'll try to break the ice with her son.' At least she could attempt to break down some barriers with the withdrawn teenager.

'Sounds great,' he said, and the expression on his face changed to one of appreciation. Sophie felt a real buzz in response to her boss's approval. 'No harm in trying, but don't expect too much. You might end up disappointed.'

Then Will promptly changed the subject, ending their conversation about Bella and her son and the future of the derelict building on the next block.

'You must be keen to see the flat.'

At the thought of a comfortable bed, Sophie felt sudden overwhelming tiredness.

'I guess I am.'

'It's only a short drive to Sabiston. You can follow me.'

'Okay.'

Sophie glanced across at Will, who was concentrating on changing stations on his car radio. His face was blank. What was going on in his head? What impression had her unconventional intrusion into his life made? Their lives were so different. He appeared to be a very private person, not bound to convention or what people expected of him.

She could live with that.

Then she thought of Bella and her introverted son and realised how small her problems were in the grand scheme of things. She felt humbled and even more determined to make a go of it.

CHAPTER THREE

SOPHIE followed in her own car as Will headed west towards the coast. The scenery transformed as soon as they crossed the railway line. Grey-slabbed roadside pavements and graffiti'd walls of grubby corner shops made way for expansive, grassed road verges, quiet streets lined with jacaranda trees and suburbs dotted with slick shopping malls.

Sophie hit the brake pedal as Will indicated to turn into the narrow driveway of a two-storey block of about a dozen art deco flats clustered around a neatly kept garden and a small brick-paved car park. The neighbourhood reeked of old money and good taste.

The surrounding residences were large and palatial without being ostentatious. The neighbouring property was a prime example—a rambling old house with an immaculately kept grassed tennis court and a garage nearly as big as Sophie's old flat back home. It reminded her of her parents' house in Manly.

She eased the car into the last remaining resident's space as Will climbed out of his car and walked across to open her door.

'I just need to collect the keys.' He gestured in the general direction of the neighbouring house. 'Do you want to meet your landlord?'

'Okay.'

'He's a colleague of mine and we went through medical school together. Andrew Fletcher. He's one of the top cardiologists around town.'

'He must be doing well for himself,' she said.

'Yeah, I guess so.'

Sophie deduced they weren't great friends. She couldn't be sure but she thought there was a hint of bitterness in Will's voice, though he didn't seem the type to be jealous of those better off than him. They walked silently up the long drive to the front door. Sophie noticed the camera above them as Will rang the bell. A gravelly voice grated through the intercom. There was the sound of several other people talking and laughing in the background.

'Will, I was expecting you earlier. We're round the back by the pool. Let yourself in the side gate and come and join the party.' The camera swivelled like a giant reptilian eye. 'And great to see you've brought such a gorgeous-looking friend.'

'Party?' Sophie was confused.

'I knew nothing about it. I just told him I'd call in to get the keys some time this afternoon.'

Will opened one side of a pair of heavy wooden gates and then he politely followed her through to the party where they were greeted by a man Sophie assumed to be Andrew Fletcher.

'So you must be my new neighbour? How delightful to meet you.' The bare-chested man still dripping from the pool briefly glanced at Will before holding out his hand to Sophie. His grip was a little too firm and he held her hand a little too long. 'I'm Andrew Fletcher. Sorry—I didn't catch your name.'

He had the lean, muscular build, dazzling blue eyes and classically honed features of a Hollywood movie star. Looks designed to catch any woman's eye—and he knew it.

He was eerily like Jeremy in both looks and manner, and the similarities made Sophie feel uncomfortable. She glanced across at Will, hoping for some indication from him as to whether to take this larger-than-life show pony seriously. Will's expression suggested he disapproved of the man's blatant flirting as much as she did.

'Sophie. Sophie Carmichael.' She desperately tried to stop her voice trembling but didn't quite succeed. To her surprise, Will responded to her uneasiness by moving close, grasping her hand and giving it a reassuring squeeze.

'Great to meet you. I hope…' his fleeting look in Will's direction barely acknowledged his presence '…you *both* will come and at least have a drink with me and my friends.'

Andrew's manner tripped a switch for Sophie and she felt nauseous. She couldn't control the sudden churning in her gut as his roving eyes played havoc with her emotions. She wanted to tell him to back off, but she didn't want to offend Will or his friend.

'The party's only just starting to warm up,' he said with a grin.

She liked the man less with each word he uttered.

This stranger was a double of Jeremy, and she had a sudden compulsion to leave before the nagging nausea in her gut got any worse.

It was then he must have noticed Will's protective gesture. Obviously not used to being rebuffed, Andrew leaned close, his breath smelling of seafood and alcohol.

Without thinking what she was doing, Sophie shrank away from Andrew and snuggled a little closer to Will. His body felt warm, strong, secure…and sexy. He made her feel safe, cared for, protected…in a way Jeremy never had.

Whoa… What on earth had come over her? He was her boss. They'd known each other barely a couple of hours and were merely acting out a charade of being more than colleagues.

She pulled away and stole a quick look at Will's face and saw a twinkle of amusement in his eyes.

'Sophie and I have other plans, haven't we?'

He was rescuing her. It was as if he had read her mind and had decided to play the knight in shining armour.

'I...er...'

'Well, you *are* a dark horse, aren't you, mate?' Andrew winked and slapped Will on the back in a misguided gesture of friendship. He'd added his own interpretation to their show of intimacy.

Will also recoiled from the man, and his grip tightened on her hand in a subtle indication of new-found solidarity. Andrew prattled on, completely unaware of the undercurrents between the two of them.

'I had no idea.' Andrew's attention firmly focused on Will, the look on his face bemused but curious. 'How long have you two—?'

'We met years back.' Sophie interrupted, trying to think quickly and say something that wouldn't exaggerate the untruths. 'And Will has kindly offered me a job for a couple of months at a time when I need to get away from Sydney.' She attempted a look, implying that was all the information she was prepared to give.

'Ah. I see. Will's playing the good Samaritan.'

Will's free arm found its way onto Sophie's shoulder and his facial expression turned into one of exaggerated concern. She was relieved when he finally spoke.

'We appreciate the offer. Perhaps another time.' He hesitated, sending Sophie a look. 'So if we could just get the keys...?'

'Okay, I'll be five minutes,' Andrew said as he loped off towards the house.

'What was that all about? For a minute there I thought you were going to faint.'

Will dropped Sophie's hand and stepped back from her, folding his arms across his chest. He looked as confused as she was. His tanned cheeks were flushed and the understanding in his eyes a moment ago had turned to bewilderment. She could already tell he was a man who liked his world to stay in a predictable orbit, but Sophie was as surprised as Will at her reaction to Andrew Fletcher.

'It's difficult to explain,' she finally said.

'I'd like you to try.'

'It's just…'

'What?'

How could Sophie explain her reaction? Why she'd needed such a dramatic out from Andrew's advances? He reminded her so much of Jeremy—charming, handsome, generous, rich, but not capable of fidelity—it was scary. In the end, Jeremy's unfaithfulness had been their undoing.

When had he fallen out of love with her? The fact that he might never have loved her had left Sophie feeling totally gutted. She'd been used—put on display like an expensive accessory and then discarded when he'd become bored with her and traded in for a new model.

Andrew was cast in the same mould.

But all men weren't animals… Not if her instinctive reaction to Will's kindness was anything to go by. It made it even more difficult for her to explain her impulsive behaviour. She figured she had nothing to lose, though, by telling the truth.

'He reminded me of my ex.' She couldn't help the grimace.

'Oh.' Will seemed uncomfortable with the direction the conversation was headed. Too much information? Too personal?

As Will dropped his arms to his sides Andrew walked through the French doors.

Grabbing Will's hand again, Sophie said in a pleading voice, 'Do you mind? He's coming back.'

Will smiled, apparently with renewed understanding and what Sophie thought was a hint of empathy. 'Just this once, but after we leave here—'

'I know. I'm sorry. I owe you for this.'

Andrew returned at that moment, handed over the keys to Will and grinned.

'I'll let you two go off and get reacquainted, then.'

He waved them off, then added as his eyes did another quick

but obvious head-to-toe appraisal of Sophie, 'Remember I'm next door if you need anything.'

'I'm sure she won't,' Will said brusquely as he put the keys in his pocket.

What on earth was it about Sophie Carmichael that had made him behave in a totally irrational manner? wondered Will.

They walked down the driveway of Andrew Fletcher's house, Sophie's hand still enfolded in Will's protective grip. She offered no resistance and he was reluctant to release her cool, tense fingers. He knew he should. Sophie was probably thinking he was taking advantage of her vulnerability.

But it felt so natural, comfortable...and so sensual.

Oh, God.

What had happened to his well-ordered life?

Will had totally lost his bearings. His day had started out simply enough. Not surprisingly, he'd been tired. It had been a busy week and 'tired' seemed to be his default setting these days. The usual Saturday morning at the clinic, demanding work, but nothing he couldn't handle, had been predictable.

It had been after morning surgery, when Sophie Carmichael had crunched, strode and then nudged herself into his life that his world had tilted on its axis.

In the space of a few short hours she'd roused the full spectrum of his emotions. He'd tumbled through frustration, amusement, impatience, confusion and...desire.

Desire? He'd almost forgotten it existed.

'That went well,' Sophie said as they reached the end of Andrew's drive.

'You think so?'

Will reluctantly released her hand and dragged his mind back from what was turning into a totally unachievable fantasy. Thank heaven she had no idea what he was thinking.

Sophie smiled. The comment was probably her way of saying how uncomfortable the encounter with Will's colleague had been for both of them. Will already had an idea what made this fascinating woman tick. She was naturally intuitive, dangerously unpredictable, and seemed to act at times solely on impulse.

And he liked it, he grudgingly admitted.

She'd also shown good judgement in her reaction to his successful, good-looking colleague. Andrew normally had any pretty woman he set his charismatic sights on under his spell in less than five minutes.

But not Sophie.

'You've obviously known Andrew for a long time but…and I might have got the vibes wrong…you don't seem to be best mates.'

She was dead right. But what could he say? He could hardly burden her with the traumas of his past.

'You're pretty close to the mark. But I didn't mean to—'

'No need to apologise. If he's anything like my ex-fiancé…'

The words stuck in her throat and her cheerfulness drained away as rapidly as the healthy colour in her cheeks.

Will felt totally at sea. Talking about problems on a personal level, especially with a woman, wasn't something he did. At least, not outside his consulting room. What was the point? It wouldn't make what had happened all those years ago go away.

But Sophie looked so dejected, as if she carried deep sadness inside. He couldn't just jump into his car and drive away without showing he cared. And, much to his surprise, he *did* care. A lot.

'Andrew and I haven't got much in common now. Our career paths diverged years ago and I guess we're both busy with all our commitments.' He cleared his throat. 'Er…what was it about Andrew that reminded you of your boyfriend?'

They were approaching Sophie's flat and Will rummaged in his pocket for the keys. He stopped on the doorstep and waited for Sophie's reply.

'Um…it's difficult to explain.' Her eyes lost focus for a moment but then she continued. 'I thought he loved me but it turned out...' She swung her gaze back. The pain was there in her eyes, hot and cruel. 'It turned out he was a first-class bastard.'

It only took a moment for a rampant blush to flood her face and she began to stutter. 'N-not that...um... It's not that I think your friend...'

There was no way Will would use the word 'friendship' in the same sentence as Andrew Fletcher after what he'd done. But Sophie didn't need to know that. She had her own demons to deal with.

'I mean, Andrew might be a nice guy... It was just a gut feeling... I'm sorry.'

Will felt awkward, not quite sure what to say. He wanted desperately to comfort her, offer reassurance, but he'd been out of the social scene for so long... Giving her a hug was probably totally inappropriate, and he certainly didn't want her to think he was cast in the same mould as Andrew. He respected his women friends and had decided long ago if he ever embarked on a serious relationship again it would be for life. And that certainly wasn't going to happen any time soon. The baggage he carried was too heavy to share.

To disguise his discomfort he unlocked the door, and the heaviness of Sophie's mood lifted.

'There you go,' he said, stepping aside. 'Furniture's basic, but you should have everything you need. I've left some supplies that I hope will keep you going until you have a chance to go shopping. There's a deli—you probably saw it as we turned in from the main road...'

He still stood on the threshold, but Sophie had waltzed in and in two short minutes claimed the place as her own. She'd opened the kitchen blind and exclaimed at the quaintness of the small private garden on her back doorstep. She'd sat on the couch and plumped the cushions before smelling the small spray of freesias he'd put in a sauce bottle on the tiny gate-leg table in the corner.

'Did you do this?' she exclaimed as she opened the cupboards and then the fridge.

Youth and happiness, untarnished by life's encumbrances, glowed on her face. The mood was contagious and Will wanted the moment to go on for ever.

'I guessed what you might need. Don't worry about throwing things away. Just give the non-perishables back to me if they're unwanted.'

'No. Everything's perfect. I love it.'

She was back in the doorway, reaching out for his hand again, but this time like an excited child. 'What are you standing outside for? Come in. The least I can do is make coffee.'

Damn, he had a meeting with a builder.

'No. I have to go. I—'

Her expression changed. Was it disappointment?

'Oh, of course. You're a busy man and you must have commitments on the weekends.' Her eyes were questioning. He was sorry how quickly Sophie's mood had changed. 'I'm sorry to have taken up so much of your precious leisure time. I'm sure your family...'

What leisure time? What family?

Lately nearly all Will's time away from the clinic had been consumed by his efforts to get his pet project off the ground. Any sort of social life was out of the question and he had no family demanding his attention. Will's heart clenched shut at the memory of the family he'd once had.

The family he'd lost, the family he'd failed...the family he'd destroyed.

And now... The residents of the Springs had infiltrated his life to become his kin. He'd long been aware that the older generation who had known his grandparents kept a watchful eye on him. And the young—the children of his adopted extended family— were the driving force behind his desire to do everything he could to give them the opportunity to achieve their full potential.

Could he ever repay his family?

He'd long ago realised the neighbourhood he'd been brought up in was the only place he felt truly at home. He'd be asking too much to expect Sophie to understand, her background being so different from his.

'No need to worry about family commitments. I'm unattached—no rug rats keeping me awake at night.' He feigned cheerfulness to disguise his loneliness.

The already rosy colour in Sophie's cheeks darkened and Will wondered what had made her blush. Did his single status make a difference? Maybe she would feel *safer* if he was married, considering what she'd just revealed about her ex-fiancé. Or did she consider him dating material?

Surely not.

His brow involuntarily crinkled in a frown as he dismissed the thought as fantasy. He rearranged his face into a smile. 'I've enjoyed your company, and any other time I'd love to share a coffee...' He glanced at his watch and then cleared his throat, wishing he could stay a little longer with Sophie. 'But I have a meeting with a builder for quotes on the renovations of the hall at the community centre.'

Sophie was silent for a moment.

'Right,' she said. 'Maybe another time.'

'Maybe.' He hesitated. 'I'll see you nine o'clock Monday morning, then.'

'I'll be there.'

As he walked to his car, Will was struck by the discomforting revelation that he was looking forward to it—looking forward to Monday morning, the beginning of another long working week... and the opportunity to see Sophie Carmichael again.

In fact, he could hardly wait.

CHAPTER FOUR

MONDAY, Sophie's third day in this strange new city, and she still felt jet-lagged. She forced herself to start her day early, and while munching her way through a couple of slices of toast reflected on the events of the weekend.

Despite the shaky start, Sophie's luck had turned—for the better.

Saturday afternoon she'd made it to the shops just before closing and bought toiletries, a change of underwear, an over-sized T-shirt for sleeping in and a simple and conservative shirt-dress that would suffice for work if she was still without her suitcases.

It was with a sense of relief that she wasn't locked into the image of well-groomed sophistication that was expected in Sydney. She'd made the right choice in leaving most of her de-signer suits and dresses at home because she doubted the newest trendy styles or the fashion label you wore had any credibility in this town, where most families had barely enough money to buy food and keep roofs over their heads. She'd already realised your credibility was more about the kind of doctor you were and how you related to those people, like Bella Farris, who deserved to be treated with respect.

Which got her thinking about her boss.

The brooding, deliciously mysterious Dr William Brent...

Already he'd proved to be a caring, insightful and forgiving employer. The fact that he seemed to have a mission in life to improve the lives of the struggling people of Prevely Springs had got her thinking…about fundraising. She'd had a few ideas floating around in her head, and when she'd written them down it was quite a list. At the first opportunity she planned to present her thoughts to Will, with the offer to take on board the organising. She felt excited at the prospect.

She'd received some good news on Sunday afternoon as well. Her luggage had finally been located and was on its way to Perth via Brisbane and would be available to pick up in the morning.

Guiltily she'd imposed again on her boss's good will and asked for some time off to collect it.

'Take the whole day,' he'd said, almost nonchalantly. 'I've waited so long for some help, another day won't make any difference.'

She'd thanked him but hoped she wouldn't be tied up all day.

She'd also had time to clarify what she wanted from her short stay in Western Australia and define some simple rules to try and ensure the next few weeks went as smoothly as they possibly could.

She was in the ideal place, working with people who didn't know her, to cast off the shackles of her past. She would shed labels like 'ditzy', 'selfish' and 'impulsive' and replace them with 'sensible', 'hard-working' and 'well organised'.

Firstly, she'd embrace the work at Will's practice with professionalism and enthusiasm. She'd concentrate on the positives and endeavour to learn as much as possible. Realistically, her stay would only be six weeks—time enough for the storm at home to have passed and for people to forget and move on to the next scandal.

Secondly, she'd have as little impact as she could on her employer's generous good nature and prove to him she could be independent, self-sufficient and an asset rather than a liability.

And, thirdly, she'd steer clear of any personal relationships.

She'd made the journey west to recover from one disaster and she wasn't about to launch into another.

That was the plan. With minimal variables and few distractions. Easy.

Feeling confident and empowered, busy and productive, she picked up her luggage from the airport and even had time to do a little shopping.

When she finished her morning business it was lunchtime, so she headed back to the flat with a week's supply of groceries, a slab of fresh-baked *focaccia* bread, a bag of fruit muffins and a packet of her favourite coffee. The plan was to have lunch, change her clothes and head out to Prevely Springs to spend a couple of hours meeting the staff and familiarising herself with the clinic layout, computer system, the protocols and procedures. Of course, if she saw Will she would treat him with the friendly respect he deserved.

After eating and flipping through Will's information booklet, she went to the bedroom and spread the contents of her suitcases on the bed. She shed her casual clothes and chose tailored charcoal-grey trousers and a smart, snug-fitting, soft pink and muted grey striped shirt. She glanced in the mirror on the back of the bedroom door, happy with what she saw—conservative, practical and just right for her first day at the office.

She fastened her shoulder-length russet-coloured hair with a beaded clasp at the nape of her neck, smeared clear gloss on her lips and then sighed.

'Let's get on with it,' she muttered.

Mondays were always busy. The clinic, theoretically, had an appointment system. Patients who just rolled up knew, unless it was an emergency, the minority who booked took precedence. What purists might have seen as unmanageable chaos worked reasonably well for the clientele of Prevely Springs Medical Clinic. The patients understood they would usually have to wait but they also knew Will Brent was a hard-working, caring doctor who would never turn a genuine patient away.

Will was sitting in his consulting room at three in the afternoon, trying to snatch a bite to eat between patients, knowing the waiting room was overflowing. He'd also promised to call in and see a baby who'd just been discharged from hospital after treatment for bronchiolitis. After that he'd check on Bella Farris. His working day wouldn't be finished until well into the evening. He frowned as he sipped tepid tea and his frown deepened as the phone rang.

'It's Sandie.' Will wished he felt as cheerful as his receptionist sounded.

'Yes.'

'Thought you might like a fresh cup of tea.'

He sighed with relief. If that was all she wanted...

'Great. Thanks.'

'And there's someone to see you.'

Will suppressed his impatience. Pharmaceutical representatives always seemed to call unannounced when he was busiest. He lowered his voice.

'Sandie, I really haven't got time to—'

'Trust me. This is someone you'll be happy to see.'

She hung up the phone and a few minutes later stood in his doorway with two steaming cups and a plate of delicious-looking muffins on a tray. Behind her...

Sophie Carmichael grinned. Will didn't know whether to laugh or cry. He'd organised to meet her early the following morning to show her the ropes and settle her in. He just didn't have time today. Though he couldn't deny the pleasure he felt at seeing her again, looking like she'd just stepped out of the fashion section of a career-woman's magazine, he wondered why she'd turned up a day early. Another mini-catastrophe? She seemed to attract them like iron filings to a magnet.

'Hello, Will.'

She sat opposite while Sandie cleared a space for the tray.

'I'll leave you to it, then,' the receptionist said. She threw a conspiratorial glance at Sophie.

'Sophie.' He forced a smile as he leaned across his desk and extended his hand. At any other time he'd have been pleased to see her, but now... It must have shown on his face.

'Don't look so worried, Will. Drink your tea while it's hot. I'm here to help.'

'To help?' He gulped a mouthful of his drink.

She handed him a muffin.

'Sorry. I'm really busy. I'd love to chat and show you around but I haven't the time. Tomorrow morning—'

'It's okay. Your very efficient and competent nurse Lisa's already shown me most of what I need to know. And Sandie's asked around the waiting room and at least half of your patients are happy to see me. I should have time to do the home visit as well and be back before you set off to see Bella Farris.'

She broke off a piece of cake, popped it into her delightful mouth and wiped a crumb from her blouse. For once he was speechless. He needed time to absorb what she'd said.

'I want to talk to Brad, remember?' Sophie paused, waiting. 'If that's okay with you, of course.'

He finally spoke. 'You want to work, see patients now?'

The long and mundane afternoon that had stretched ahead was suddenly filled with light. Sophie was the first ray of sunshine to break through dark clouds after a storm.

'That's right. And Sandie's kindly told your next one you'll be at least ten minutes.'

'Oh.'

'So you may as well make the most of your break and eat.' She smiled. 'The muffins are scrumptious.' She seemed happy to cheerfully carry on the conversation alone. 'And that sandwich looks disgusting.'

He obediently took a bite of the cake and she was right. Delicious, just like her smile. He felt the tension in his body begin to melt away.

'I found this wonderful hot-bread shop on the way back from sorting out my luggage. Pity it's not close by...' She paused in mid-sentence and studied his face for a moment. 'Are you all right?'

'Yes. I'm fine.'

If you discount the peculiar lightness in my head and the urge I have to take you in my arms, kiss you thoroughly and swear my undying gratitude.

'You've made my day.'

'Good. If it's okay with you, I'll start helping to clear the waiting room.' She took a sip of her drink and then stood as if to leave, but waited—apparently for his permission.

'Yes, of course. If you're happy to—'

'I am.' She looked at her watch. 'You officially have six more minutes left of your break so I suggest you make the most of it.' She turned in the doorway. 'And if I'm not back by the time you finish, give me a ring. If you haven't got my mobile number, Sandie has it. I can meet you at Bella's.'

And with a delightful swish of her hips she was gone.

Working in Will's practice was like stepping into another world for Sophie. Although her afternoon went smoothly—the patients who had elected to see her had fairly straightforward problems— she'd noticed the majority of people she'd seen were...*so different* from what she was used to. They'd learned not to bother the doctor unless they were genuinely, seriously ill. Wasting her or Will's precious time meant someone who legitimately needed attention was put further back in the queue. And even though most couldn't afford the sort of fees her father's patients paid, there'd been a sense of heartfelt gratitude from several people she'd seen that could never be measured in dollars. It was almost as if the people of the Springs were used to being rebuffed by authorities purely because of their social status. They considered time spent with a doctor who was prepared to listen and take their problems seriously a privilege rather than a right.

For the first time in a long time Sophie felt the beginning of a return in the confidence and drive she'd had as a new graduate when she'd been ready to take on the world. In hindsight, her self-esteem had probably been eroded over the past two years without her even realising—by Jeremy. He'd never taken her career seriously, and had considered her work to be only a convenient and lucrative means to keep her happy and occupied until they married and started a family.

And her father was just as controlling. When he had realised she was determined to have a career in medicine he'd decided, without even consulting with her, that his practice, under his watchful eye, was where she should stay. She'd been shocked to overhear him talking to Jeremy about maternity leave and reducing her hours when the grandchildren started coming along—as if she had no say in the matter.

The fact that Jeremy's new girlfriend was pregnant had been the final straw for Sophie. She'd tried so hard to please her fiancé, forsaking her needs for his, and he'd not shown a morsel of remorse at trading her in for a flashy new model who was going to present him with a baby long before he was ready. When *she'd* broached the subject of children, he'd seemed put out that she'd even consider taking on the responsibility of a family before he finished his specialist training in the well-paying field of ophthalmology.

It made her wonder if the little chat he'd had with her father about job flexibility and maternity leave was a complete sham. Maybe it had just been a ploy by her father to make sure she stayed in the family practice to take over when he retired. The fuss he'd made when she'd told him she'd applied for and been accepted for a job in Western Australia had been over the top. Even after she'd explained she'd most likely be back in a month or two.

Will wasn't like that.

The thought entered her mind without warning as she realised how intimately her new employer was part of what she was feeling.

She'd had her first taste of how the other half lived...and worked and suffered. It validated her reasons for coming to WA, and she was beginning to experience the type of satisfaction in her work she'd longed for.

By five o'clock the waiting room was nearly empty. Only two patients remained and they both insisted on seeing Will.

Sophie headed for the reception area. Home visits were something she'd have to get used to as they were an integral part of the holistic style of medicine Will practised, rarely encountered in city practices these days.

She breezed into the reception area with renewed energy.

'From what you told me, I shouldn't be long,' she said to Sandie.

Sophie gathered the printed notes listing the details of the infant she was going to visit, as well as the hospital discharge summary. She had her own medical bag, but Lisa had kindly put together a bundle of the clinic stationery, which, she noticed with a smile, had been freshly printed to include her name and new provider number.

'Are you coming back?' the receptionist asked.

'If Dr Brent is still here. We're going to see Mrs Farris. I met her on Saturday.' Sophie could tell by the look on Sandie's face she knew Bella and the nature of her illness. 'I can meet him there if he finishes before I come back.'

Sandie smiled. 'Will rarely finishes before seven, sometimes as late as eight on a Monday. And that's without home visits.'

'It doesn't surprise me. He's the only doctor for... How many patients did you say were on the books?'

'Way too many. He works too damned hard.'

'Mmm.' Sophie knew it too, and she'd only known him a few days. If he kept going as he was, he'd burn himself out. Her respect for him was growing by the minute. 'I'd better get going.' She gathered her gear and turned to go.

'Sophie?' Sandie's voice was quiet, kind.

'Yes. Have I forgotten something?'

'No. I just wanted to tell you what a difference you've made this afternoon. Thanks.'

'Just doing what I'm paid to do.' But Sophie knew that was never the case in medicine. To be a doctor, and especially in a practice like Will's, you had to be prepared to give that very substantial bit extra.

Sophie drove into the clinic car park half an hour later as Will walked out the back door, punching a number into his mobile phone. He stopped when he saw her.

'Perfect timing. I was just about to ring you,' he said as she stopped beside him and lowered the window. He looked a little less weary, and the hint of a smile as well as a barely perceptible spark in his almost black eyes was all Sophie needed to tell her she had been a help to him that afternoon.

'Are you going to see Bella Farris now?'

'That's right. Shall we go together?'

'Sounds good to me. Climb in.' She pointed to her passenger seat but Will looked reluctant. 'The more I drive, the more I get to know my way around the neighbourhood.'

He seemed to accept her logic, put his bag and a pile of medical journals on the back seat and settled himself next to her. 'Thanks,' he said, fastening his seat belt.

'No problem.'

'I don't just mean for the lift. You did really well this afternoon. Sandie told me a couple of patients were singing your praises.'

Sophie had enjoyed the afternoon of what was sometimes called bread-and-butter medicine. Simple problems with relatively simple solutions. So different from the wealthy patients of Sydney's eastern suburbs where she'd worked in her father's practice.

'Don't worry. I'm not about to poach your patients. Every

single customer who consulted me this afternoon let me know
they were loyal to you and only saw me because they knew you
were so busy.'

Will laughed. 'Poach as many patients as you like. Just remember when you get your own following they'll...'

Sophie knew what he was going to say and understood why
his voice trailed off.

'They'll give me a really hard time when they find out I'm
leaving?'

'Mmm. Something like that.' It was a conversation-killer;
neither of them was contemplating the future beyond the following day at this stage of their professional relationship.

'Is it left here?' Sophie asked when she thought she recognised
the street.

'Yes. To the T-junction and left again.'

Sophie turned into the quiet suburban street. A group of grinning teenagers bounced their basketball precariously close to the
car and then went running off in the opposite direction.

'Tell me about Bella. How long has she been ill?'

'Her cancer was diagnosed about three months ago. She'd had
stomach pains and what she described as indigestion for only a
couple of weeks before the scan.'

'Pancreatic cancer is often untreatable at the time of diagnosis,
isn't it?'

'Incurable is probably a better word. We can still treat the
symptoms as part of palliative care. Best quality of life is the
general aim. And then a peaceful death.'

Sophie looked across at Will but he was staring out of the
side window, a distant look on his face.

'Is Brad an only child?' Sophie understood why withdrawal
into the realm of computer games was attractive to the teenager.
In his fantasy world he probably had control and, from what
Sophie had seen, he played at a level of skill that assured he was
a winner most of the time.

'No. He has an older married sister. She lives in Karratha,

which is roughly fifteen hundred kilometres north of here, and has a young family of her own. She'll come down for Bella's last days and will take Brad back to live with her and her husband.'

Sophie recognised the group of townhouses as they turned the corner and she eased her car into the ragged driveway of the Farrises' house.

'Brad's father?'

'A drunk and a bully, so Bella told me, and long gone. She doesn't know where he is and doesn't want to. He'd left before I started seeing Bella.'

'She cares about Brad, though.'

'Yes, she does. His future is her biggest concern at the moment.' He paused and looked at her with narrowed eyes. 'Perceptive of you to see that.'

'I guessed, that's all.'

'Yeah, well, you guessed right.' Will got out of the car and then leaned into the back seat to get his bag. 'Come on. Let's go.'

Will knocked and then opened the door, calling out as he did so, 'It's Dr Brent and Dr Carmichael. Can we come in?'

He didn't appear to expect a reply, and when they entered the house the TV was on but Brad was in the kitchen, stirring the contents of a saucepan on the stove.

'Hi, Brad.' Will nodded towards the boy.

'Hi.'

'Smells okay, but you didn't have to go to all that trouble.'

Brad smiled, then went back to stirring.

'Mum said she feels like some tomato soup.'

'Good. She must be a bit better. Has Shelley been?'

'Yeah.'

'And? Did she say anything?'

'Nothin' much.'

Will slouched against the brick pillar supporting the wall

dividing the living area from the kitchen. He gave the impression of having all the time in the world.

'Don't give me that. Shelley'd talk the nuts off a prize stud bull.'

Brad's smile turned into a grin for a moment.

'She said Mum's a bit better.'

'Good.'

'And that I'll end up as fat as her if I don't stop eating rubbish.'

'Ha.' Will's eyes twinkled. 'Now, that's a scary prospect.' He went over to inspect the soup and crinkled his nose. 'You won't get fat on this. We'd better go up and see your mum,' he added.

Brad put the lid on the pan, turned off the hotplate, and hovered as if waiting for them to make a move.

'Come on, Dr Carmichael.'

When they went upstairs and into the back bedroom Sophie could see the improvement in Bella—her smile was less forced, her colour better and her face not so lined with pain. A half-drunk glass of milky liquid stood on the bedside table.

Will picked up her chart and spent a few moments looking through the nurse's notes. 'Nausea's settled?'

'Yes, and the pain. That little pump works like magic.' Bella pulled aside her pyjama top to reveal the butterfly needle inserted under the skin of her chest and the battery-operated pump that slowly and steadily moved the plunger of the syringe to administer a constant supply of pain-relieving medication.

'Are you keeping any food down now?'

'A little. I've opened my bowels too.'

Will looked over at Sophie and explained, 'Hopefully the dexamethasone has begun to act to reduce gut inflammation and swelling.'

'Whatever. It's working,' Bella said.

'Good. Can I examine you?'

Bella dutifully lifted her top.

'Do you mind if I go downstairs and have a chat to Brad, Mrs Farris, while Will checks you over?'

'Call me Bella. I don't mind. But he doesn't talk much. Seems to spend most of the time when he's not at school playing electronic games.' A look of sadness crossed her face. 'His friends don't come over any more. I wish...'

'He seems a good kid. He was making soup when we arrived.'

It was the only way Sophie could think to reassure the woman whose mood had taken a dive when they'd started talking about her son.

'He is.' She hesitated. 'I wish things were different.'

Sophie glanced at Will, wondering if her decision to try and find out how the boy was coping was a wrong one. He nodded his approval.

'I guess we can only do our best with what we've got.' The comment seemed totally inadequate in the circumstances.

'Yes, you go and talk to Brad.' Bella's smile returned. 'And good luck.'

Will heard the laughter as he came downstairs, and then a whoop from Brad followed by Sophie's less animated groan. They were both sitting on the couch. Sophie's eyes were glued to the TV screen and her thumbs were on a game console control pad as if it was an extension of her hands.

'Ooh.' Sophie's voice was a little louder this time, easily heard against the background noise of racetrack engines revving and squealing brakes. 'Gotcha!' She threw her head back and laughed for a second, then her eyes shot back to the action on the screen.

'Watch out. Ha!' Brad exclaimed, and by the look on his face he was obviously winning the computer racing driver game.

Will stopped to take in the sight of Sophie. With her privileged upbringing, she was an attractive, sophisticated career-woman, and yet she was currently playing with young Brad with the enthusiasm and lack of inhibition of a child. Will hadn't seen Brad laugh like that since his mother had been diagnosed with incurable cancer. Even before Bella's illness he'd seemed an introverted, though intelligent kid, content with his own company.

Though he wasn't sure where Sophie was going with Brad, the boy was enjoying himself, which was an enormous positive step. As long as she didn't let him get too close to her.

'What's the game?' Will stood behind them at the bottom of the stairs. Neither had been aware of his presence.

Brad's head shot round.

'Mario Kart, out of the archives.' It was Sophie who answered.

'Am I supposed to know what that is?'

'Nup.' Brad was still engrossed in the action on the screen.

'Is she any good?'

Brad glanced briefly at Sophie before he answered. 'Not bad for a girl. But she's played before.'

Sophie put down her control pad and let her driver succumb to the inevitable humiliation of coming last in the race.

'I remember when computer games had only just been invented. The Mario Brothers games were my favourite. I've got a kid brother,' she said, as if that explained everything.

Will had never been a fan of computer games, and Sophie's comment reminded him of his age. He was nearly a decade older than she was.

Sophie got up to leave. She tapped Brad on the shoulder.

'I might come sometimes when Dr Brent visits your mother. Is that okay, Brad?'

'Okay.'

'And don't forget your mum's soup,' Will added.

'I won't,' he said as he turned the machine off.

Will and Sophie let themselves out and walked to the car.

'That went well,' Will said.

'It did, didn't it?' Her eyes glistened in the fading light. 'I think I might have made it to first base with him, but his biggest challenges are yet to come.'

Will knew exactly what she meant, but he suspected Sophie might be the one to make his journey a little less painful.

'I don't know how you did it, but you managed to put a smile on Brad's face,' Will said as he climbed into the passenger seat of Sophie's car.

'I played a computer game with him, that's all.' Sophie positioned herself in the driver's seat. 'And maybe my inner child's a bigger part of my psyche than in the average grown-up.'

Will laughed. 'If that's what it takes to get Brad out of his shell, I'm all for it.'

Sophie reversed out of the driveway. The street was quiet, no cars or people. The only sign of life after dark in this eerie place was the occasional flicker of a television screen seen through a curtainless front window and the sound of a distant barking dog. So different from Sydney, where even the suburbs seemed alive with folk going out to restaurants, walking dogs, visiting friends. It was as if by some mutual agreement the residents of Prevely Springs observed a curfew. If Brad felt isolated, Sophie could understand why.

'It's only the first step with him and I have no idea what the next one will be.'

'But you've made a start. That's more than I've managed.'

'Mmm.'

They drove in silence to the end of the road. Sophie didn't need directions this time. The maze of streets was beginning to look familiar.

'How much time do you think Bella has left?'

'Not long. Maybe a month—two at the outside.'

'She knows that?'

'Yes. We've talked about it. She's already put her affairs in order, made plans for Brad, that sort of thing.'

'Does Brad know?'

'He knows his mother's dying. We had a family conference a few weeks ago. Her daughter Gemma travelled down from Karratha. I didn't think it was fair to talk in terms of *how many weeks*.'

'No, I guess not.'

They drove past the park, part of the community centre complex. A restless group of youths had gathered under a streetlight, pushing and shoving each other. One lunged towards the car, pulling a face and making an unsavoury gesture until he saw Will. Then he smiled sheepishly.

'You know him?' Sophie asked.

'I know most of them. Always in trouble, mainly because they've no direction. Nothing else to do. In a different situation...' Will seemed to focus on some place in the distance.

'At least Brad isn't roaming the streets.'

'Yes. That's one positive, I suppose.' He sighed.

Sophie sensed Will had a bond with the people of Prevely Springs that went deeper than the doctor-patient relationship. There was only so much one person could do, though.

She stopped the car outside the clinic.

'Do you want to share some take-away?' she said on impulse. Will looked so despondent.

'No, thanks. I have a couple of things to finish off.'

'Work?'

'If I don't do it now—'

'Never leave until tomorrow...'

'That's right.' He opened the rear door to retrieve his gear, a look of determined acceptance on his face. 'You know how to get back to the flat?'

'I'll be fine. See you in the morning.'

Will smiled. 'Yes. I will, won't I? It's great to have you on board, Dr Carmichael.'

'My pleasure,' she muttered, easing her car away from the kerb.

Those two words weren't a clichéd reply. It was the absolute truth.

CHAPTER FIVE

'WILL works too hard,' Sophie said to the two women in the tea room. It was Friday lunchtime, after a busy morning consulting, and Sophie's observation was partly due to the fact her boss was working through his lunch-break...again.

'Tell me something we don't know,' Lisa replied as she removed the cling wrap from her sandwich.

'And he's taken on much more than he can possibly handle with the youth centre. Has he mentioned it to you?' Sandie addressed her question to Sophie.

'Mmm, on my first day, when we went and saw the Farrises.' Sophie took a sip of coffee. 'We were talking about Brad, and Will was lamenting the lack of facilities for young people in the neighbourhood.'

'He's right about that, but one man can't move mountains. Apparently the council have told him he has to show he can raise a six-figure sum before they'll even consider his proposal, let alone approve it. And it's not as if the residents have any spare cash to give away.'

'Has he said how he plans to do it?' Sophie had been mulling over her own ideas all week but hadn't had a chance to discuss them with Will.

'Apparently he has some well-to-do colleagues he was going to ask to sponsor the project, but he didn't seem too overjoyed at the prospect,' Sandie volunteered as she went across to the

kettle to refill her cup. 'When it comes to the Springs, he seems
to want to shoulder the entire load himself.'

'Mmm—he's not someone who's comfortable with the cap-
in-hand role.' Lisa chuckled. 'We were all amazed he finally
decided to take on an extra set of hands.'

The women carried on eating and drinking in silence until
Sophie decided to share her thoughts, find out what Sandie and
Lisa thought about her wanting to help.

'I have a few ideas.'

Her companions looked at her with surprise.

'To raise a couple of hundred thousand dollars?' The look on
Lisa's face turned to incredulity.

'Like to share them?' Sandie pulled her chair a little closer
and put down her cup.

'I wouldn't mind sounding you out on local knowledge but
I'd rather run them by Will before I...' Sophie grinned '...go
public.'

Sophie had a feeling that if she told Lisa and Sandie the details
of her plans they'd be common knowledge before the day or at
least the weekend was out. She wasn't ready for that yet, and she
doubted the residents of Prevely Springs knew her well enough
to trust her. The proposals had to come from Will.

'Are the youngsters around here into sport?'

'Playing or watching?' Lisa asked.

'Both.' Sophie could see she had the women's full attention.
'Any particular sport?'

Sandie and Lisa exchanged curious glances before Sandie
answered.

'Aussie rules footy, I guess.' She looked at her friend for con-
firmation and Lisa nodded. 'You probably know there are two
national teams in the West, and I'd say the majority of the football
supporters around here go for the port team.'

'The underdogs.' Sophie had enough knowledge of the sport
to know of the rivalry between the two West Australian teams
and that the Fremantle team, though not usually as successful

as their opponents, had an incredibly loyal following. 'Are there local amateurs? Do the kids play?'

'Pete, my husband, plays for the local team and coaches both boys and girls in the under-twelves.' Lisa paused. 'Where are all these questions leading?'

'I'm not sure yet, but you've been a great help.' Sophie grinned. 'Just one more question. What's the spectator capacity of the Springs sports ground?'

Lisa answered. 'I'll ask Pete. The local team never plays to a big crowd but at full capacity it would be around a couple of thousand at the most.'

Sophie looked at her watch.

'Thanks, ladies. I'd better be getting back to work.'

The information Sophie now had gave her more to think about, and by the looks on Sandie's and Lisa's faces she'd given them food for thought as well.

Sophie packed her things at the end of the Friday afternoon session. Her first week had been busy and she was looking forward to a relaxing evening—a long, hot shower, a supersized serving of her favourite take-away, and then watching back-to-back crime shows on TV.

She was just about to leave when the phone rang.

'Hello?' she said a little impatiently, hoping the call wouldn't lead to a delay in the start to her weekend.

'Thank goodness you're still here. I thought you might have left already.' There was no mistaking the urgency in Sandie's voice.

'What's the problem?'

'I wondered if you could see one last patient.'

'An emergency?' Sophie's heartbeat quickened and the muscles of her neck and shoulders tensed.

'Not exactly.' Sandie hesitated.

'Go on.'

'It's a woman who normally sees Will, but he's still got four patients in the waiting room. I buzzed him and he didn't want her turned away. He okayed you seeing her as long as you let him know if you have any problems.'

'Right. I just need a few minutes to log back into the computer. What's her name?' Sophie resigned herself to missing at least the first half of *City Crime*, but hoped the rest of the evening would go to plan.

'Beverley Sanders. And…er…she's got her daughter Brianna with her. Dr Brent said to tell you to check Brianna's notes as well.'

'Okay. Tell them I won't be long.'

'Thanks. You're a lifesaver.'

Sophie replaced her bag in the file drawer at the side of her desk, locked it and put the key in her pocket. She sat in front of the computer screen and waited the few seconds for it to reboot, then logged in with her password and entered the medical records.

Beverley Sanders…

Age thirty-one—the same age as Sophie. In fact, their birthdays were within a few weeks of each other. Marital status—de facto. Three children aged four, seven and fifteen. History of depression and a coded reference to her having been a victim of domestic violence.

Her life hadn't been a bed of roses.

The woman had seen Will a fortnight ago, and the brief notes alluded to a long consultation about problems she was having with her oldest daughter. He had requested she bring Brianna along when she saw him in a week's time.

The visit obviously hadn't happened and Sophie had a good idea why. Fifteen-year-old girls with difficult behaviour rarely admitted to having problems at all, let alone came willingly to attend the doctor for help.

Sophie did a quick calculation—Beverley had been sixteen when she'd had Brianna.

She did a check of the teenager's notes. The entries were

sparse—a note documenting her refusal to have the rubella or the cervical cancer vaccine; three stitches in her forehead a year ago after a fall—Will had underlined that—and an entry a fortnight ago referring to her mother's visit: *'Problems at home with Brianna—?drugs'*.

Will had mentioned to Sophie that drug use and abuse was a big problem in the neighbourhood, and increasingly among high-school kids. He'd drilled her in what to look out for and how to question teenagers without being threatening or intrusive. He'd revealed that helping these youngsters was a special interest for him.

Sophie took a deep breath. Clenching her hands into fists to stop a slight tremor, she headed for the waiting room.

'Beverley Sanders?' she said. She glanced at the waiting patients but they were all male. Had Beverley and her daughter decided not to stay?

'Sandie?'

The receptionist was on the phone. She grimaced, then pointed to the front entry, before miming the action of drawing on a cigarette.

The message was clear. Her patient had gone outside for a smoke. The prospect of Chinese food and a quiet, relaxing evening was gradually fading as Sophie realised these last two patients would almost certainly take time. A lot of time.

Sophie walked across and opened the front door.

'Beverley Sanders?' she repeated, this time louder.

A woman emerged from behind the open driver's side door of an old car, stubbing out a cigarette as she slammed the door shut. She was overweight and dressed in the most unflattering cropped stretch pants, topped with a sleeveless, scoop-necked T-shirt at least a size too small. The outfit accentuated her obesity. Her straw-coloured hair straggled over her shoulders and her neck was swarthy and lined from too much exposure to the sun.

She hammered on the windscreen.

'Come on, Brianna, the doctor's waiting,' she shouted, and

LEONIE KNIGHT   69

then shrugged an apology to Sophie. 'Sorry—you've no idea what it took to get her this far.'

The woman looked desperate...and weary, as if, with every choice she made in her life, she ended up with the short straw.

There was something about the look in her eyes, though, that indicated she was a survivor and wasn't about to give up. She deserved all the help she could get, Sophie decided.

Beverley hit the windscreen again and a thin girl Sophie surmised was Brianna emerged with a sour expression on her face. Sophie suspected the challenge she'd been wishing for had just arrived on her doorstep and was about to shuffle into the clinic scowling and under protest.

Sophie smiled her warmest welcoming smile.

'I'm Dr Carmichael. You must be Mrs Sanders?'

The woman nodded.

'And Brianna?' The girl looked away and said nothing, but ambled behind her mother in the direction of the clinic doors.

'Challenging' was an understated description of the fifty-minute consultation that followed.

'What brings you here today, Beverley?' Sophie's usual opening line sounded totally inappropriate and even a little snobbish. She felt the woman withdraw a fraction before she glanced at her daughter, as if to make sure the girl hadn't absconded.

'I've had it with Bri.'

'I told you not to call me that,' the teenager snapped. 'My name's *Brianna*.'

'See what I mean? She's like that all the time. But a lot worse. Arguing, shouting, swearing like a loser about the tiniest thing. And then she'll sink into a dark mood and won't talk to me or her stepdad for days. She went into a flaming rage a couple of weeks ago and slapped her little brother for changing the TV channel. That was the last straw.' Beverley was bravely holding back tears. 'The bruising on Joel's face lasted a week.' She paused and then added quietly, 'She used to be such a beautiful, well-behaved little girl.'

Sophie looked over at Brianna, who was still scowling and restlessly tapping one heel on the floor.

'Go on.'

'She sneaks out at night, falls asleep in class or doesn't show up at school at all. She's been suspended twice for smoking dope…and if it happens again she'll be expelled.'

'Okay.' Sophie needed a minute to organise her thoughts. She was determined to at least try and help.

'Brianna?' She'd surprised the girl. Brianna looked as if she didn't expect to be included in the conversation. 'Are things at home difficult for you too?'

The girl's facial expression relaxed for a moment, but then went straight back into rebellious teenager mode.

'What difference does it make?' she muttered.

'I'm not sure, but I think it would be worth trying to find out.' Sophie made sure she kept her tone neutral. It would be a big mistake to take sides. She fixed her gaze firmly on Brianna, but her question was directed at her mother as well. 'Would it be all right if I had a chat to each of you on your own? Maybe starting with you, Brianna?'

Beverley stayed silent, so the decision was up to the fifteen-year-old, but the girl was obviously reluctant to agree with a suggestion made by an adult on principle.

'What's the point?' she finally said. At least she'd acknowledged the question.

'We won't know until we give it a try.' Sophie glanced over at Beverley, who nodded her approval, looking relieved.

'Well?'

'Yeah, okay.' It was almost a whisper.

'Good.'

Her mother was standing already.

'If you sit in the waiting room, I'll call you when we've finished.'

Beverley walked wearily to the door and closed it softly behind her.

Challenge number two was about to begin.

The six-thirty call from Sandie, telling Will that Beverley Sanders had finally fronted up with her daughter in tow, had been unexpected. That the girl had come at all surprised him, and he could only imagine the effort her mother had made to persuade her. He had to see them. There was a good chance he might not get another opportunity. He often worked well into the evening when he was theoretically supposed to finish at six.

'Sophie's seeing her last patient and you've got another four waiting. Would you like me to ask her if she can see Beverley Sanders and her daughter?'

The receptionist had cleared her throat. Sandie had worked with Will since he'd first set up the clinic, over ten years ago, and had a good knowledge of the backgrounds of their regular patients. He assumed she already had an opinion of what their new assistant could cope with. In fact, a young, fresh, female doctor might be what Brianna needed to open up. His suspicions, from what her mother had told him, were that the teenager was experimenting with harder drugs—he knew all the tell-tale signs first hand—but he was interested in Sophie's assessment.

'As long as Beverley is agreeable.'

'And I'll tell Sophie you're in the next room if she needs any help.'

Sandie had amazing insight.

'That's exactly what I was about to say.'

'Good. I'll buzz you if they refuse to see Sophie.'

That had been nearly an hour ago. Will had finished consulting, but Sophie's door was closed, which meant she was still working. He wasn't sure whether to be worried or impressed, and was keen to know the outcome of the visit.

He'd wait.

And he didn't have to wait long.

As he began to go back to his office Sophie's door opened and Beverley and Brianna emerged.

'Hello, Dr Brent.' Although she wasn't smiling, there was a sense of relief in Beverley's body language. Her daughter, shoulders hunched and head down, looked at the floor. She seemed calm, though, not agitated or angry, as he'd expected. 'I hope you don't mind us seeing the new doctor.'

The apology was unnecessary and he smiled.

'Of course not. We work as a team.'

'Good. Dr Carmichael wants us to come back next week.'

'Make sure you make an appointment before you leave.' Will smiled. He wanted to reinforce the fact he had no objections.

Brianna started heading towards the waiting room but Beverley looked as if she had something more to say. Sophie's door was still open, but from where Will stood, a little past her office, he couldn't see her. She could probably hear their conversation, though, which was the most likely reason Beverley leaned close to whisper, 'That woman's a gem. Brianna actually talked to her. Make sure you do everything to persuade her to stay.'

'I'll do my best.'

The woman had a rare smile on her face as she turned to follow her daughter, and Will did an about-turn to find out how Sophie had managed to perform a miracle.

Sophie hunched over her desk with one hand supporting her head and her gaze directed at the computer screen.

Will knocked quietly.

'Sophie?'

She sat up and swung round abruptly on her swivel chair, looking surprised. Perhaps she *hadn't* been aware of the conversation taking place in the corridor. She ran her fingers through her hair. She had beautiful, shining hair, a rich reddish brown with glints of coppery gold when the light caught it in a certain way. She'd left it loose, and he liked it better that way than tied or clipped back, her usual style for work. He imagined it would be soft to touch and sweet smelling.

Her hand went back to her head, flicking stray strands behind her ear.

'Is there something wrong with my hair?' She was blushing and he reprimanded himself for blatantly staring. He hadn't realised…

'No.'

Everything was right with it.

'Sorry. I…er… It's been a long day,' he added—a lame attempt at justifying his behaviour.

'I know you've had a long day, Will, and I won't keep you—I'm sure you've got plans for the evening—but I wanted to have a quick word about Brianna Sanders before the weekend…to make sure I've done the right thing.'

Plans for the evening? Right. Buying a take-away on the way home and falling asleep watching TV after an aborted attempt at making an impression on the pile of journals in the corner of his study.

Of course he had plans.

'As a matter of fact I haven't any plans for tonight.' He moved one of the patient chairs back so he could sit facing her without his knees tangling with hers. He'd just had an outlandish thought. 'Have you?'

She grinned. 'Take-away and an early night. I think I'm too tired for anything else.'

'Do you like Chinese?'

'It's my favourite.'

'How about we share a Chinese take-away and go back to my place…?' He hesitated, but Sophie showed no sign of protesting. 'Or yours, if you prefer. And we can discuss your first week, as well as Brianna Sanders, on a full stomach.'

'That sounds good to me. I've got a couple of things I want to talk to you about.' She did her best to suppress a yawn. 'I can't guarantee I'll stay awake, though.'

'Not a problem. My house has two spare bedrooms.'

Whoops. He hoped Sophie didn't put the wrong interpretation on his invitation for a sleep-over. But she seemed oblivious to any inappropriate implications.

'Your place, then. I'll follow you in my car, but you'd better give me the address just in case I get lost,' she said as she unlocked the drawer to retrieve her bag.

Suddenly Will was no longer looking at the prospect of another dull evening at home on his own. He felt energised, with a feeling of lightness replacing the heaviness that usually encompassed his entire body towards the end of his working week.

Maybe it was time to at least consider there might be a life for him outside his job. He somehow put to the back of his mind that Sophie Carmichael was out of bounds.

Sophie couldn't deny she was curious to see where Will lived. She felt comfortable with him. He was so conservative she doubted he had an ulterior motive; her problem, though, was that she kind of wished he had. She felt certain that somewhere beneath his sombre, sober, serious exterior he hid a sense of humour. She'd had glimpses of it but he usually kept it well hidden.

The weird thing was she wanted to be the one to crack his shell. The idea had come on her slowly through the week and left her surprised and confused. She'd fantasised about showing him the therapeutic value of letting his hair down and having a good time.

He was the sort of man who probably didn't understand the meaning of the word flirting. It most likely hadn't occurred to him that if he smiled a little more often, if he wore more flattering clothes, if he even thought about asking a woman out, he'd be inundated with attractive ladies eager for his company.

There was something holding him back, though. Maybe something in his past he wasn't able to let go of. Perhaps he'd suffered the female equivalent of Jeremy. Someone who hurt him badly. Whatever, whoever it was it had a firm hold on him.

But at the moment he was probably just as weary as she, and needing an uncomplicated end to a hectic day. She put thoughts of trying to analyse the man out of her mind.

Sophie followed Will to a busy Chinese restaurant and he insisted on her helping to choose their meal.

'My place isn't far from here,' he said as he loaded several containers of delicious-smelling take-away into his car. Sophie followed him along the main road and then into a narrow brick-paved street softly illuminated by old-fashioned lamps. The street was still in or at least on the edge of Prevely Springs, but had a character all its own.

The row of Federation houses, though built to the same plan, were each different. One had a bright blue front door with lace curtains and white miniature roses falling from a muddle of terracotta pots in the front yard. Another was all trendy grey paint and shiny black security screens. Sophie pulled up behind Will as he parked in the driveway of the last house in the row.

Will's house.

It surprised her, but it suited him somehow.

The small garden of straggling native plants had found their own special state of disorder. They softened the façade of the old stone building, which stood aging but proud and defiant. It quietly declared its protest against modernisation.

Will was out of his car and leaning towards her window.

'This is it,' he said, almost apologetically.

'I like it. It's so—'

'Don't you dare say quaint.'

'No.' She smiled. 'I was going to say it's so *you.*'

He grinned. 'I won't ask if that's meant to be a compliment or an insult.'

Will went back to his car, collected the food and then led her through a faded picket gate with a predictably squeaky hinge, up the low stone steps onto a dusty veranda. She could just make out intricately patterned tiles in the muted colours of earth and sky. It was like walking back in time.

'How long have you lived here?'

Will unlocked the door, flicked on the hall light and then turned to face her. 'Nearly my entire life, I guess. It was my grandparents' house. I spent a couple of years travelling...' He hesitated, as if deciding whether to continue.

'And?'

'The first two years of my life I lived with my mother. But I don't really remember...'

His voice trailed off and he gave her a look that told her he didn't want to talk about his past.

'Come through to the back and we'll eat.'

Sophie assumed he'd been brought up by his grandparents but didn't delve further. She followed him down the central passageway. The dark, closed-in front of the house opened up to a paradoxically light and airy, open-plan kitchen and informal living area.

'I'm responsible for the extension,' Will said, as if he needed to explain. 'I love the old house but it was time for change.'

Despite the contemporary features—a full wall of timber-framed glass doors, pale, polished wood floors, modern kitchen appliances—it all somehow blended with the history of the place. The furniture was a mix of old and new: a modern sofa; two antique high-back chairs; an ageless rocking chair.

'Sit down.' Will indicated the sofa. 'I'll bring plates and you can serve yourself. Okay?'

'That's fine.'

'Would you like some wine?' He opened the fridge, checking the contents. 'Or beer?'

'No, thanks, but don't let me stop you.' She'd be asleep before she finished her meal if she had even one drink.

'I'll just have water, I think,' Will said as he selected a bottle of spring water from the fridge. 'Okay?'

'Perfect.'

The meal was tasty and satisfying, and Will sustained an easy conversation, explaining the operation of his medical practice, discussing staff and a few of his more challenging patients.

He cleared the plates and returned with two cereal bowls heaped high with ice cream. A bite-sized chocolate bar was jammed into each serving.

'I won't be able to move if I eat any more.'

'Just eat what you can. I won't be offended.'

'I'll do my best.'

They ate dessert in silence, until Sophie could eat no more. She put her bowl on the table and pushed it away.

Will leaned over for her dish. 'I'll make coffee.'

Sophie snatched it away. 'No. You've done enough. I'll make coffee while you finish your ice cream.' She smiled. 'And then we can talk about Bev and Brianna.'

Sophie stood in the kitchen—his kitchen—with her back to him, washing dishes and making coffee.

She looked so at home.

Had it been such a long time since he'd entertained a woman that he'd forgotten what it was like?

But Sophie wasn't just any woman. He hadn't spent the last week working with her with his eyes closed. But there never seemed to be a spare moment in the day at the clinic where he could speak to her for more than a few minutes, let alone relax and enjoy her company.

His gaze fixed on that glorious mass of wavy hair that caught the light in a magical way, so that he wanted to touch it to see if it was real. The proportions of her compact body were just right— sculpted shoulders, lean, lightly muscled limbs, gently curved spine and a perfectly rounded bottom that moved tantalisingly as she turned to put each clean dish on the drying rack.

Whoa... Where had that come from?

An abrupt awareness of his long-suppressed libido had Will's thoughts darting in all directions and totally confusing him. He wanted to run his fingers through Sophie's hair and inhale the perfume of it…of her. He imagined slowly exploring the nape of her neck with his lips and then spinning her round and grasping that adorable rear so he could pull her close. Close enough to let her know how his body was reacting.

And—oh, Lord—his body was certainly reacting. If he didn't put a stop to this totally inappropriate train of thought, he was likely to seriously embarrass himself.

He rearranged his legs, put his hands deep in his pockets and sank a little further into the soft cushions of the couch, trying desperately to think of something so boring it would take his mind off Sophie…and sex…*sex with Sophie*. Not an easy task, but it worked.

Just in time.

She'd finished making coffee and presented him with a tray laden with a steaming plunger, two mugs and a small glass jug he'd forgotten he owned filled with milk.

'You found everything?'

The front view was even more…sexy. It was the only word Will could think of to describe the glimpse of the creamy white skin of her breasts, soft and rounded, edged with peach-coloured lace that Sophie had unknowingly exposed as she'd leaned over to put the tray on the coffee table.

Sophie sat down.

'Except the sugar.'

'I spoon my sugar straight from the packet.'

'Which I'm afraid I couldn't find.'

'Oh. I think I ran out yesterday.'

The mundane conversation about his failings as a housekeeper clinched it. He could stop worrying. Uncrossing his legs, taking his hands out of his pockets, he poured the coffee. Mercifully, his only thoughts were of when he would have time to do some shopping on the weekend. And how much he needed that mug of coffee.

Sophie slipped off her sandals and settled in the corner of the sofa, tucking one foot up on the seat and arranging herself in the collection of cushions so she was looking directly into his eyes. She was so relaxed. Her life was uncomplicated, her privileged upbringing enviable, her view of the world unsoiled by the reality of the kind of life he led. She yawned.

'I'm sorry.' She giggled, as if she was tipsy with tiredness. 'I think I'm going to need this coffee or I won't last the distance. We planned to discuss Brianna Sanders.'

Her eyes closed a moment, but then opened as he put her drink on the coffee table in front of her.

'Thanks.' She reached forward and then took a sip.' Shall we get down to business?'

'Of course. Brianna Sanders.'

CHAPTER SIX

MANY of Will's patients were living reminders of his past, and he suspected he was about to add Brianna Sanders to the list. If she *was* using drugs, for whatever reason, she had little hope, without help, of fighting her way out the hole she and her so-called friends were digging for themselves,.

When Will had taken over the suburb's ailing medical practice the statistics for physical, psychological and social dysfunction as well as actual deaths related to drug and alcohol abuse in Prevely Springs had been appalling. There had been some improvement over the years Will had been working there, but he knew there was so much more that could be done—and one busy GP just couldn't do it. Not on his own.

He'd tried his best, though.

Before Sophie Carmichael had breezed into town Will had been close to giving up.

But her fresh and optimistic outlook had revived him.

Yes, she was young, naive, and a little bit flighty at times, but she was eager to work. She certainly wasn't shy of a chal-lenge either, if the time she'd spent with her last patients was any indication.

He was keen to know how she'd coped.

'So, how did things go with the Sanderses this evening?'

'That's the problem, Will. I'm not really sure. Beverley would have jumped through flaming hoops if she'd thought it would bring back the "well-behaved little girl" she said Brianna used to

be. She was receptive to every suggestion I made. But Brianna…
Trying to talk to her was like trying to milk a bull.'

Will noticed a tiny muscle twitching in one of Sophie's
eyelids.

He knew exactly how she felt. Tired and frustrated.

He sighed.

'That bad, huh?' he said. 'Bev told me Brianna's behaviour and personality changed soon after she started school last
summer, after the Christmas vacation. She was fine before then.
Does that ring any alarm bells with you?'

'I saw your note in Brianna's records about possible drug use,
so I was tuned in to it being a potential reason for her behaviour.
At first she said her main problem was she couldn't sleep and she
wanted sleeping pills. I refused and said we had to find a cause
for the insomnia before treating it, then asked her directly about
drug use. She went so far as admitting she binge-drinks with
mates but not that often. Maybe once a fortnight. She smokes
dope when she can get it as well. The insomnia sounds more like
a symptom of using uppers, but she denied taking speed or any
of the similar drugs.'

Was it Will's imagination, or had Sophie's attitude subtly
changed when she'd mentioned the drinking? He sensed a slight
increase in her muscle tension. She clenched one of her hands
into a fist and her eyes lost focus—just for a moment or two. He
was used to reading body language, and he trusted his instincts.
If Sophie had some sort of baggage related to alcohol it was
probably best he know about it—particularly in view of his own
past problems.

But she was now totally focused and back on track, and he
wanted to hear more about her encounter with Brianna.

'Sounds like you're making progress with the girl.'

'I hope so. But I reached a dead end as far as her revealing
anything more about drug use.'

'Do you think you're gaining her trust?'

'I'm trying, but we're not there yet. For the rest of the

consultation I decided not to pressure her and went along a different track. I asked if she had any plans for when she left school.'

'And?'

'She surprised me. Said she'd always liked cooking and wanted to be a chef. She'd never mentioned it to her mother, though. And it's all bound up in low self-esteem. Her stepfather keeps telling her she's a useless piece of work and he can't wait to be rid of her. He certainly doesn't want to spend any money on her education and his attitude seems to be eroding any progress Bev makes. Bev's reached the point where she's run out of energy to stand up for Brianna.' Sophie paused and took a sighing breath. 'So Brianna resorts to bad behaviour, including drug use. It's a no-win situation.'

'You think she's using amphetamines?'

'Probably. The signs are there. If she is, I can't see her stopping unless we tackle the underlying causes.'

Sophie's emotional involvement with Brianna and Bev Sanders, even after one visit, was written all over her face. The sadness in her eyes, the frustration in the frown furrowing her forehead, the bewilderment and uncertainty in her expression all touched Will's heart. His dilemma was whether to let her go with her feelings—and risk being let down—or to warn her against the hard reality that change had to come from the patient herself. All a doctor could do was try and teach the skills to make positive decisions that could turn lives around. Will had been in that dark and self-destructive place and been lucky enough to see sense. Many others didn't have the strength of mind.

He had to caution her.

He wanted to comfort her.

'Sophie?'

She stopped fiddling with a loose thread on one of the cushions and looked up.

'Yes.'

'You've done good work with Bev and Brianna, and it sounds like you've got what it takes to tackle their problems.'

'Thanks,' she said. An appreciative smile lit up her face. 'This is new territory, and it's great to have your reassurance I'm on the right track.'

This is a woman with many layers, Will thought, and Sophie was beginning to reveal that what lay below the glitzy surface was a dedicated, caring doctor and a woman who was taking his breath away simply by being in the same room—there was no other way he could think to describe what he was feeling.

He had to get his mind back on the reason she was there. To discuss a challenging patient.

'But don't get too close to the issues and problems in what sounds like a pretty dysfunctional family.'

'I'm not sure what you mean. When you're trying to help someone, it's pretty difficult not to.'

'Maintain a degree of detachment…as protection against disappointment.'

Despite her outward sophistication Sophie had a soft centre, and Will felt the need to protect her from the kind of mistakes he'd made too often himself.

'You've made a good start with her. The fact she admitted to abusing marijuana and alcohol is a pretty big step on a first visit.'

That momentary look was there again—a mix of sadness and suppressed distress that Sophie was unable to hide. Will felt a compulsion to find out what had triggered it.

'I hope you don't mind me asking…and you can tell me to butt right out…but do *you* have any kind of personal issue with alcohol, or other drugs?'

He knew what he was saying was confrontational but he had to clear the air. If Sophie had any unresolved issues…

She blushed fiery red and then looked down at her interlocked fingers in her lap. He hadn't expected that kind of reaction. Will regretted being so frank.

'I'm sorry. I was out of—'

'No, that's okay. It's not something I talk about.' She paused and her eyes reconnected with his. 'And I probably should—even though it happened a long time ago.'

'A long time ago? What happened?'

'When I was sixteen, my best friend—I'd known Jessica nearly all my life—was killed in a car accident that shouldn't have happened. Her so-called boyfriend was driving, showing off and speeding. He was breathalysed at four times the legal limit. You know the scenario. It's in the papers every day. He walked away with barely a scratch and little in the way of remorse.'

Sophie's hands trembled and her eyes shone bright with unshed tears. But she hadn't finished.

'Since then I always get edgy when I'm with anybody who drinks to the point of getting drunk.' She managed a smile. 'And I've been known to fly right off the handle at anyone who drinks more than one or two and says they're going to drive.'

Sophie's life hadn't been as charmed as he'd thought. Money certainly offered no protection against the tragedy she had experienced. Neither could it erase the memories.

Will felt compelled to comfort her.

He moved a little closer and put his hand on hers.

'I'm sorry,' he said quietly.

A single tear escaped from her brimming eyes and she wiped it away with her sleeve. Then she grasped Will's hand, pressing it to the dampness on her face. He needed no other invitation. He leaned across, put his arms around her and kissed her forehead.

Sophie was no doubt feeling vulnerable, her emotions fragile, but she was so beautiful…soft…and warm. She didn't protest or pull away but snuggled close to his neck. With the slightest tremor in her hands, she intertwined her fingers behind his head.

Will held her closer and nuzzled into her beautiful, silky, sweet-smelling hair. His lips found the corner of her eye and touched her lids gently, one after the other, until the dampness was gone.

A tiny guttural sound issued from her throat and he could feel her heart beating even faster than his own. Will wanted to consume her, but it was Sophie who opened her eyes, tilted her head a little and then pressed her lips against his open mouth.

What was supposed to be a comfort-giving hug had inexplicably turned into something much, much more.

Their kiss was exhilarating for Will; an awakening. At first it was merely gentle pressure of sensitive skin against skin, then a hesitant probing of the nectar-sweet recesses of Sophie's mouth as she opened up to his intimate caress. The hungry exploration that followed left Will breathless. As the kiss deepened Sophie's hands traced a tortuous pattern down his back until she reached the belt of his trousers and pulled at his shirt until it was free. The touch of her palms as they skimmed the skin of his lower back sent a stab of molten heat to his groin.

This shouldn't be happening!

For at least a dozen compelling reasons.

Will opened his eyes and eased himself away from Sophie, who seemed to sense his passion had ebbed. He hoped she understood.

'I didn't mean to take advantage of the situation,' Will finally said, after what felt like an interminable silence.

Sophie ran her fingers through her hair and straightened her rumpled shirt. She was still close enough for him to feel the warmth of her breath and see the gradual rise of colour from the pale skin between her breasts to her neck and then her cheeks.

The physical intimacy they'd shared had taken him totally by surprise. It was out of character, inappropriate, and wouldn't happen again.

Sophie moved away and picked up her sandals from the floor.

'I'm sorry if...' Will had no explanation as to why, but he needed to apologise.

She looked up and gave him a half-smile.

'Don't be. I was as much to blame as you.' Her smile broadened. 'I guess we're both tired, got caught up with the moment, forgot that doctors should always listen to the left side of their brains. Impulsive decisions are not our forte. No harm done.'

'It won't happen again.'

'No,' she said quietly, slipping on her sandals. She glanced at her watch, her composure having fully returned. 'It's getting late. I'd better go.'

'The offer of the spare room still stands,' Will added, knowing she wouldn't accept and not blaming her.

'Thanks, but, no, thanks. I've been too much of an imposition on you already... And I sleep better in my own bed.'

Will wasn't about to labour the point to tell her she definitely was not an *imposition*.

'I'll see you tomorrow, then.'

Sophie didn't sleep particularly well in her own bed. She kept reliving how it had felt to be enfolded in Will's gentle arms, how a comforting kiss could turn into a deeply arousing revelation of passion and how, if Will hadn't pulled away, she could have easily been persuaded to take the kiss to the next stage.

No! She'd vowed to stay away from men...from *relationships*...from setting herself up for the same mistakes she'd made with Jeremy. It was too soon; she was too vulnerable. She had to fight the feelings she was beginning to have for Will Brent with all her might.

Where had it come from—the embrace, the kiss, the wanting more? She searched her mind for a logical explanation.

Maybe from a place in her heart that had been locked for too many years.

She'd not confided in Jeremy about her friend's death. He'd never been good with *personal,* or *emotional*, or anything involving a woman shedding tears. He was a typical macho, self-absorbed male who believed life's tragedies should be dealt with promptly before moving on.

But Will was different. She'd never met a man like him. He was totally selfless in so many things he did. He was kind, caring, understanding and also...very sexy.

Had she used him purely to fill the emptiness left by Jeremy? The thought horrified her.

After making herself a mug of warm milk, trying to read a magazine and then listening to a relaxation CD, she finally fell asleep at close to three in the morning. She then slept soundly and wasn't woken by her alarm. Her mobile phone began ringing at just after seven o'clock. She fumbled amongst the debris left from the previous night's sleeplessness and finally found it.

'Hello?' She half hoped it was Will, telling her how much he'd enjoyed last night and asking when they could do it again. But the voice on the line was gruff—annoyed, even.

'Sophie?'

'Yes, Dad. Is anything wrong?' Her father had rung her twice already during the week, supposedly to check how the job was going and how his 'favourite daughter' was settling in 'all on her own'. His previous calls had been at a more civilised time, though. Sophie suspected his agenda was to check up on how Will was treating her. He didn't seem to understand how she could *choose* to work in his practice, treating people from a social demographic he mistrusted and tried his best to avoid.

'Well...er...not wrong exactly, but there's something I thought you should know.' There was no loving greeting or even a stilted enquiry as to how she was. He obviously had something important on his mind.

She sighed, resigning herself to the fact that the extra hour of sleep she'd been hoping for, due to her later start at work on Saturday morning, wasn't going to happen. She was wide awake.

'And what's that, Dad?'

'I bumped into a dermatologist at a lunchtime meeting

yesterday—someone who went to university in WA at the same time as your Will Brent. I tried to ring you last night but couldn't raise you.'

'I went out, Dad, and came home late. I left my phone in the car.' The last part was true, but she wasn't about to give him any more detail. If he asked for extra information, she'd say it was a night out to do with work. But he seemed more preoccupied with imparting his own important information. 'What did you want to tell me?'

'Well…er…' Her father cleared his throat. 'Apparently Dr Brent had problems in med school.' He paused, but Sophie stayed silent and let him continue. 'He nearly got booted out in the early years of his training—failed some exams—but was given a second chance.'

'Dad!' She was annoyed at her father's muck-raking interference and felt she had to defend her boss. 'You know nothing about what Will Brent's like, or his background. He's a good, caring doctor. He's not well off, like us, and I imagine he had a battle supporting himself while he was studying. I admire him for what he's achieved and I like working with him. It makes no difference to me whether he failed a couple of subjects.'

'I haven't finished, Sophie.' Her father's voice was now hard as steel, and she knew he had more dirt to turn. 'He was a drunk.'

'What?' Sophie couldn't believe what her father was saying. 'What do you mean?'

'He apparently had a problem with alcohol.'

She laughed. 'But what med student *doesn't* go over the top with drinking?'

He obviously didn't see the humour.

'You don't understand. He had a big problem. He was abusing the stuff—an alcoholic. The only reason he was allowed to continue studying was because he vowed to give up drinking completely.'

Sophie felt tears brimming. Why was her father telling her this? Through some misguided sense of protection?

'Okay, you've said what you wanted to say. I have to go now, Dad. I need to get ready for work. I'll keep in touch,' she added out of politeness, and then pressed the 'end call' button. If her father thought she was being rude, that was his problem.

Sophie had agreed to work alternate Saturday mornings. Having an extra doctor, even for only a couple of hours, was a godsend for Will. He told himself so a dozen times as he tried desperately to put Sophie Carmichael and that exquisitely sensual kiss out of his mind.

'Oh, God, what have I done?' he muttered.

He had no room in his life for a woman…and definitely not Sophie. He had nothing to offer her. And he had no right to lead her on, even in the name of a brief affair. He didn't do affairs. He'd tried it a couple of times and the result had been anger and tears.

Should he talk to her? Or just pretend it hadn't happened?

As he drove into the clinic he still hadn't made up his mind.

Half expecting her to be tight-lipped about what had happened the previous evening, he wasn't surprised that after a polite 'Good morning, Will,' she hurried off to her room.

He saw little of her after that, and it was small consolation that her coolness, at least for the time being, solved his dilemma of whether to confront her.

But he wanted to clear the air. The fact that what he'd offered as purely a hug of reassurance had turned into something much more was regrettable.

Though at the time he'd certainly felt no regret. He'd been so caught up in the bombardment of physical sensations and long-forgotten emotions he'd just wanted to hold Sophie—beautiful, tempting, sexy Sophie—in his arms for ever.

The thought of revealing how he felt frightened him.

He'd dreamed about her last night. She'd floated into his

bedroom wearing a pure white, gossamer, full-length nightgown. She'd sat on his bed and offered him her hand, saying, 'Take me now. You might never have the chance again.' But when he'd reached for her hand she'd disappeared—like all the beautiful things in his life, all the people he'd really cared about, she had been snatched away.

He couldn't face that happening again—he had to talk to Sophie before she left.

Amazingly, they'd run to schedule—it was only just past midday, and the waiting room was empty, so he assumed Sophie had finished as well.

As he went to find her Will's mind whirled with twenty different ways of explaining and apologising for taking advantage of her vulnerability the previous night.

She was in the treatment room, tidying up after a procedure. He knocked softly, and when she turned she forced a smile.

'What can I do for you?' she said casually.

'I need to explain about last night.'

She resumed her task of clearing the trolley. 'There's no need, Will. Forget it ever happened. It was the result of a set of unexpected circumstances. Nobody's fault. Let's just leave it at that.'

She'd summed it up perfectly. The kiss had meant nothing. *He meant nothing to her.* He tried to hide his disappointment but she was right.

'As long as you understand…and as long as it won't affect our professional relationship.'

'Of course not. See you next week,' she muttered.

She pushed past him, the brief touch sending a pulse of bright heat through his veins. Will wondered how he would cope with the next few weeks—not because of overwork, or tiredness, or the constant demands of his patients, but because of working side by side with Sophie… Unfathomable, untouchable Sophie.

He sighed. Why was life so complicated?

CHAPTER SEVEN

WILL was in a good mood. Sophie was proving to be a real asset
to the practice. She'd been seeing more of Will's regular patients,
which had definitely eased his workload. The clinic income was
picking up as well—partly due to news of a female doctor in the
neighbourhood spreading to the women in the area, particularly
the older ones, who were reluctant to see *him* for any problem
that might involve 'intimate women's complaints'.

He began wondering how to persuade her to stay. Purely for
the benefit of the practice, of course.

He was trying his best to ignore the fact his relationship with
Sophie had subtly changed since that unexpected kiss a week
ago—without much success. He'd begun viewing Sophie more
as an attractive, very feminine woman rather than simply as a
colleague.

Despite his determination to keep their relationship on a professional level, it had become increasingly difficult to treat her
purely as a very able assistant as she settled into the routine of
working in his practice. He found himself at times behaving
quite irrationally. He ironed his shirts; he'd resurrected a bottle
of aftershave he hadn't used for years; he'd even tried to restore
some order to the chaos that was his desk. And he'd been sure
his face had turned cherry red when Sophie had caught him
staring at his reflection in the tea room window, attempting to
rearrange his unruly hair.

'If you're trying for the rugged, tousled look, you've definitely succeeded,' she'd said with a laugh.

He'd been unable to come up with a witty reply so he'd simply said, 'I just realised I'm overdue for a haircut.'

Sophie had grinned and sashayed out of the room, leaving him confused.

So when Andrew Fletcher's secretary rang one evening, to invite him and Sophie to one of Andrew's famous dinner parties, he'd had mixed feelings about whether to accept. Sophie would benefit from meeting some of the local specialists, but he knew how uncomfortable she'd been in the company of Andrew during their brief encounter when they'd collected the keys to her flat.

There was also a compelling reason for Will to attend. It presented the ideal opportunity to talk to some of Andrew's wealthy friends about raising money for his project. A possible complication of them going together, though, was that it would perpetuate the pretence that he and Sophie were a couple. Will wasn't good at acting, and dreaded having to explain to Andrew. He'd also have to make it clear to Sophie it wasn't a date.

The first thing he needed to do was check with Sophie before accepting and now, Friday lunchtime, was the ideal opportunity.

'Sophie!'

The sole occupant of the tea room, she had her head bowed over a journal with a steaming mug at her side. She glanced up with a look of mild surprise on her face. Will rarely had time for breaks, and he realised, guiltily, that he hadn't managed to have lunch with the staff since Sophie had started working with him.

'Mind if I join you?'

'No, of course not.' She closed the journal and took a sip of what smelled like real, fresh-brewed coffee. 'Can I make you one?' She stood before he had a chance to stop her. 'I bring my own and brew it in a plunger.'

'I'd love one. I'm not that keen on instant either, but—'

'I know. You need spare time to make it and, more impor-
tantly, to enjoy it.'

She was dead right, Will thought as he watched her swish
the grounds, depress the plunger and pour him a mug full of the
drink he thrived on.

Sophie had her back to him, and when she reached up to
get the sugar from an overhead cupboard he was treated to a
delightful glimpse of thigh and an accentuation of the curve of
her bottom under her snug-fitting skirt. He sighed.

'Busy morning?'

Fortunately she'd totally misinterpreted his admiring response.
She brought his cup to the table and sat down.

'Steady, I guess. I certainly haven't been rushed off my feet.'
He hadn't yet told Sophie how much difference her working with
him had made. 'I can't remember the last time I had a proper
lunch-break. It's thanks to you I'm beginning to enjoy the luxury
of having some spare time.'

'That's great to hear.' She seemed to accept the compliment
graciously, but moved on quickly. 'Have some.' She pushed a
plate of what remained of some lightly toasted rolls and savoury
pastries towards him.

'I saw Brianna Sanders yesterday, and I was hoping to see
you today for your opinion,' Sophie said.

'Well done. You must have struck a chord with her. Bev didn't
hold out much hope that she'd co-operate. Any progress?'

'I think so, but it's hard to tell. I don't want to send her running by accusing her of using, let alone abusing illegal drugs.
I'm still trying to gain her trust.'

'Sensible move.'

'I spent thirty minutes with her just talking about the problems of being a teenager. You know—bossy, controlling parents,
annoying younger sibs, school, boys, sex. She really started to
open up—until I asked her if there was a drug problem at her
school.'

'And?' Will was impressed with her approach. For someone

with her social background Sophie had remarkable insight into how Brianna's mind worked.

'She reverted to one-syllable answers so I wound the consult up and asked her to come back next week.'

'From what you've told me, you're on track with her. In my experience with kids like Brianna, the most important thing is getting their trust. After that, it takes time and lots of patience. They eventually start listening and accepting that the advice you give isn't all rubbish just because they perceive you as being too old to understand.' Will took a second bite of a mini cheese and spinach quiche. 'This is really good.'

'I know. I ate way too much.' Sophie looked at her watch and stood up, pushing her chair under the table. 'And I'd better get going. I think I'm fully booked this afternoon.'

'One last thing, Sophie.' Will hadn't touched on the main reason he wanted to see her.

'Yes?'

'I had a call yesterday from Andrew Fletcher's secretary.'

The tiniest flicker of a frown creased her forehead.

'He's having a dinner party next Saturday night. Apparently a gathering of colleagues. He wondered if you and I would like to come. His secretary said Andrew thought it might be helpful for you to meet some of the local specialists—put faces to names, that sort of thing. I think they call it networking these days.'

Sophie took a few seconds to process the information, but her reaction was difficult to read.

'Tomorrow night? It's a bit short notice.' she said.

'No, the following Saturday.'

'Oh.' She hesitated. 'Are you going?'

'I honestly haven't decided.' He paused, carefully considering what he would say next. 'Obviously it's not a date...but if you want to go, and you don't want to arrive on your own, I'd be happy to accompany you. I'll probably know most of the people there.'

'And you'd be a buffer between Andrew and me.' She smiled.

'If you like.' He smiled wryly in return.

'What time?'

'Between seven-thirty and eight.'

'Okay.' Her eyes suddenly lit up. 'It could be a perfect way to plug our…er…I mean your cause.'

She was thinking along the same lines as him, but her enthusiasm for a task he wasn't looking forward to surprised him. The last thing he'd expected from his new recruit was willing involvement in his obsession with rescuing the derelict building down the road in the name of trying to aid a group of young people many would regard as beyond help.

'I'll come round to the flat and we can walk across together.' Will grinned. An otherwise long and boring evening in the company of Andrew and his cronies might turn out to be pleasurable…with Sophie as his companion.

'Okay. It's a date.'

Will was frowning. She'd said the wrong thing, mentioning the word *date*, which made her even more nervous at the prospect of telling Will about her ideas for fundraising. She had no valid reason to be anxious, though. After all, Sandie had wheedled information from her a week ago and had done a lot of the groundwork—information-gathering, the compilation of lists of potential participants and donors. Her local knowledge had been invaluable. And now Sophie was eager to share their secret with Will. They already had a solid, workable plan. But not much time.

She summoned up the courage to say, 'Have you got a minute to spare? There's something else I want to talk to you about.'

Sandie breezed in as Will looked at his watch.

'You won't believe this. Your first patient's cancelled and there's no one waiting.' She paused, and looked from Sophie to Will and back again, then grinned.

'Am I interrupting something?'

Will looked suddenly awkward.

'Of course not.' Sophie had the feeling she was rescuing her boss. 'I was just going to discuss our…er…research over the past week.'

Sandie's face lit up with a smile of anticipation.

'I wondered when you'd finally summon up the courage,' she said with a wink. 'I have a couple of minutes. Mind if I stay?'

Will looked more and more bewildered as their conversation continued. But he remained silent. Sophie sat down again.

'That would be great.'

'What's all this about?' Will finally said, after noisily clearing his throat.

'The community centre.'

Sophie held her breath, wondering what her boss's reaction would be to what some might consider meddling.

'I have some ideas for raising the money you told me you need.'

Will smiled indulgently. Sophie could tell he wasn't taking her seriously—probably thinking she was about to propose selling raffle tickets or chocolates at the front desk.

'Go on,' he said, with eyebrows raised questioningly.

Sandie sent her an encouraging glance.

'It's just an idea, but I thought of a football match.'

'A football match?' Will seemed to be trying his best to suppress a laugh. 'Remember we need to raise nearly a quarter of a million dollars.'

'Listen to her, Will. She's done this kind of thing before. You'll be surprised,' Sandie said with a knowing look.

Sophie took a deep breath. 'The idea is to reach outside the district—attract people who have money to spend and offer value for their hard-earned cash.'

Will listened attentively so Sophie continued.

'The national league season doesn't start for another six weeks, and there's interest from both teams in playing a practice match—like a pre-season derby—before the competition kicks off.'

'How do you know?' Will's interest was increasing.

'I contacted both teams' publicity departments and actually spoke to one of the coaches,' Sandie contributed with a grin. 'Of course, the media has got so much mileage out of...er.... the transgressions of one of their high-profile players they seem keen for a diversion that will show the clubs in a good light.'

'And where would this match be held?'

'The local ground is way too small, but I have three dates we could have East Park's oval free of charge. Two of those days, Sunday the twelfth or Saturday the eighteenth, are possibilities for both teams.'

'Free?'

'It's all in the marketing. If you can convince them it's free advertising—'

'You *have* done this before,' Will interrupted.

'Once or twice.' Sophie grinned and then went on. 'The capacity of the ground is ten thousand, give or take a couple of hundred. At ten dollars a ticket, plus some celebrity packages, the sale of food and drink, as well as a fashion parade and an auction, that would be at least half the money you need. The rest, I hope, will come from corporate and individual donations.'

'Fashion parade?' The expression on Will's face was one of disbelief.

'At half-time. That is where I really shine. You have to believe me—I know about fashion.'

'Sophie's already got tentative involvement from— What's the latest tally?' Sandie was as excited as Sophie.

'Sixteen.'

'Sixteen boutiques around the city and inner suburbs. They'd donate clothes. We plan to get local teenagers to model them, and then auction them. And Sophie's confident we can obtain just about everything we need, including insurance, as donations.'

Both women stopped talking and looked expectantly at Will, who seemed overwhelmed.

After an interminable pause Will spoke.

'You think you can organise an event of that scale in...' he seemed to be doing a quick calculation in his head '...four or five weeks?'

'Of course. Having a deadline's part of the buzz.'

Will frowned and Sophie suddenly felt all their hard work in the last week had been wasted. She should have realised her conservative boss was unlikely to take on an event of such magnitude.

But then his face broke into a grin.

'What the heck? Go for it, girls.'

Sophie now had official approval to get things moving and it needed to happen fast.

'Where's the boss?' Sophie asked Sandie on her way out of the clinic at the end of the afternoon session. The waiting room was empty so she assumed Will had finished for the day.

'House call and then he's going home,' Sandie said as she picked up the phone, which never stopped ringing.

Sophie waited for her to finish her conversation before continuing. The receptionist turned on the answering-machine.

'I want to organise a meeting.'

'When?' Sandie was sorting patient records ready for filing the following morning.

'As soon as possible. I was hoping for tomorrow afternoon— say, about two o'clock? I've already checked with Lisa, and she and Pete can come as long as we don't mind her youngest tagging along.'

'Suits me. I have nothing else planned.' She grabbed her handbag from under the desk and extracted a bunch of keys. 'Doug said he could help with the building side of the project and has some ideas. Would it be all right if he came too?'

Sophie smiled. She could feel the momentum building already.

'The more the merrier,' she said. 'I'll contact Will tonight and only let you know if it's not a goer.'

The women left the building together.

'See you tomorrow afternoon,' Sandie said with a wave.

When the phone had rung the previous night, just as Will had been taking the first large bite of pizza, his initial reaction had been one of dismay. Although he employed a locum service to cover emergencies after hours, he'd made it quite clear he wanted to be contacted if there were any problems with his patients. In effect, that meant he was available seven days a week.

But hearing Sophie's voice had instantly lightened his mood. Her enthusiasm was contagious and even if he'd wanted to, he hadn't been able to refuse her invitation to what she called 'a planning meeting', which would be held on Saturday afternoon.

When he opened the door to the tea room at twenty minutes to two the following afternoon he was greeted by Sophie's vibrant, twinkling eyes and disarming smile. She was alone and leafing through a large folder. Looking at her, all flushed cheeks and cheerfulness, infused him with a wonderful feeling he couldn't quite define. In the mix there was definitely hope—something he'd almost forgotten existed—with a good dollop of anticipation and a large pinch of…pleasure. Yes, there was no doubt he was pleased to see her and wished he could claim her company all to himself.

'The others should be here any minute,' Sophie said as she gestured towards the chair next to her.

'Who else is coming?'

'Sandie and Doug, Lisa and Pete, as well as a good friend of Doug's called Charlie Mundy and his daughter Colleen.'

Will swallowed hard and then cleared his throat. Charlie had been one of his grandfather's best mates. Will had gone to school with Colleen and she was now a teacher at the local high school. Since the death of Will's grandparents Charlie had always been there for him—if ever he needed a confidant, a shoulder to cry on or just someone to talk to who understood.

'Why Charlie?' The question had to be asked.

'I hope you don't mind, but from what Sandie told me he'd be a great bridge to the people we're trying to help. He apparently has widespread contacts in Prevely Springs so he's volunteered to be our community liaison person.'

Before Will could reply, Caitlyn appeared in the doorway.

'Okay if I go now? All the filing's done and I've switched the phone over, so hopefully you won't be disturbed.' She paused at the sound of chattering people approaching the back door. 'Looks like the team has arrived.'

'Off you go, then, and enjoy the rest of your weekend,' Will said.

A few moments later the room was filled with a noisy mob carrying plates of sandwiches, steaming meat pies and an enormous chocolate cake. Lisa busied herself with boiling the kettle and Sandie introduced Sophie to Charlie and Colleen, who were both beaming, then Colleen approached Will and gave him a hug.

For a few seconds Will was overcome with emotion.

He was no longer alone.

Surrounded by true friends, he was suddenly aware they were as passionate about the future of the Springs as he was. By his side sat the woman who had made it happen—the woman who was, as each day passed, quietly permeating nearly every aspect of his life; the woman he could very easily fall in love with...

The realisation struck him like a blow to his chest. He felt winded, unable to breathe, as his heart thudded in his chest.

No! He mustn't let it happen. Love led to one place only—a dark, hurtful torment of disillusionment. His grandparents had loved him—and he'd been their ultimate disappointment; he'd loved Tanya with all his being—and she had been snatched away; he'd dreamed of another kind of love, a mother's love, but he knew his dream would never come true.

'Is something the matter, Will? You've turned deathly pale,' Colleen said as she stepped back from him.

All eyes turned to him as he found his breath.

'I'm fine.'

Sandie chipped in. 'You're working too hard...and I bet you missed breakfast this morning.' She piled a plate with food and pushed it towards him. 'Am I right?'

'About breakfast, yes,' he said as he selected a sandwich. 'The food looks fabulous.'

Content with his answer, Sandie summoned the attention of the group and they all got on with the business of how to turn the fortunes of Prevely Springs around.

The meeting went better than Sophie expected.

They formed what could loosely be called a committee, with Sophie and Will sharing the helm, Sandie taking the jobs of treasurer and fashion parade co-ordinator, Doug volunteering to round up volunteers to help on the day, and Lisa and her husband taking on organising the football match. Colleen, as well as liaising with the neighbourhood schools, was put in charge of publicity, while her father was to be the voice of the committee in the community.

A good deal of the initial groundwork had been done, and Sophie had no doubts in her mind that their close-knit team would turn Will's dream into reality.

She sighed as the excited group collected the debris of a very busy and productive afternoon and left Will and herself to tidy up a couple of loose ends.

Will looked totally exhausted.

'Do you want another coffee?' she said as she put a bundle of papers in her bag.

'No, thanks,' Will replied.

He slumped back into the seat he had recently vacated to say goodbye to the rest of the crew. He looked...in need of a hug. Sophie resisted the temptation.

'I won't keep you long. It's just the issue of…er…petty cash. There'll be expenses along the way that we can't expect the committee to take care of,' she said.

'Of course.'

After Will offered Sophie a paid afternoon off a week in the lead-up to the event, and a generous cash amount to start the ball rolling, he got up as if to leave and then hesitated.

'Sophie,' he said, and the weariness in his eyes was replaced by what she thought was a spark of appreciation.

'Yes?'

'I just want to thank you. You have no idea—'

'There's no need. I've enjoyed every minute…and what else would I do in my spare time?'

She smiled and Will took a step towards her, looking danger-ously, enticingly attractive. He stood motionless for a moment and then lifted his hand to touch her cheek before grazing his fingers along a burning line to the angle of her jaw.

She wanted so much for his lips to soothe, his fingers to caress, his body to meld intimately with hers. But he dropped his hand and stepped away, leaving Sophie bewildered. How could such a simple touch leave her so…aroused? Had he any idea…?

'Sorry… I didn't mean to…'

Of course he knew, and was feeling just as vulnerable and out of control as she was.

But yielding to her gut feelings, to her body's reaction, was out of the question.

She stuttered a reply. 'N-no…no, of c-course you didn't. You must be tired. You must be… *I'm* sorry…' By now she was burn-ing hot all over and her heart had gone into overdrive. She leaned down to pick up her bag in an attempt to hide her embarrassment, but only succeeded in dropping it and scattering the contents over the floor.

Will grasped her shoulders and spun her around so her face was mere centimetres away from his. She closed her eyes, not

sure if it was in anticipation of a kiss or to block out the smoul-
dering desire in Will's eyes.

Oh, Lord, I want this so much.

CHAPTER EIGHT

IT HAD taken all the self-control Will could muster to stop himself enfolding Sophie in his arms, pressing his impatient body against hers and kissing her thoroughly.

The situation had been awkward to say the least and could have easily turned into a monumental blunder...if his mobile phone hadn't rung.

Saved by the bell.

His conversation with the locum doctor had brought them both back to reality, and Sophie had taken the opportunity to make a hasty exit while Will was still on the phone.

Neither of them mentioned the incident through the week, though Will had half expected Sophie to bow out of their dinner engagement with Andrew Fletcher. On Friday, he reminded her of the dinner party and she said she was keen to meet Andrew's friends and hoped they were generous as well as wealthy.

She continued to tackle the fundraising project with gusto. He sometimes wondered why she was prepared to offer so much at the same time as giving him the impression she was having a ball doing it. After a great deal of thought he'd finally decided to not question her motives and let her, and Sandie, and half the population of Prevely Springs get on with the task of bringing Sophie's ambitious plans to fruition.

So when Will arrived home after work on the afternoon of the dinner party his mood was buoyant. For the first time in years he felt...happy, optimistic, and confident of a positive future for himself and the people of the Springs. He was on a high that had nothing to do with mind-altering drugs, but an awful lot to do with Sophie Carmichael.

He hummed softly as he showered. Then he pulled on a T-shirt, a pair of faded knee-length denim shorts and cast his gaze downwards to take stock of himself—something he rarely had the time or inclination to do. In fact, his house didn't even boast a full-length mirror.

He frowned. The casual crumpled look was definitely no longer fashionable.

The shorts, trendy in their day, were at least ten years old. The T-shirt, black with the graphic of a 1980s rock band emblazoned on the back, could probably only redeem itself as a collector's item.

But what did it matter? He wasn't trying to impress anyone, was he?

An image of Sophie popped into his mind. She seemed to be having an impact on him in many unexpected ways. He reluctantly admitted *she* was the reason he was thinking about clothes. And for some scary reason he didn't understand, it mattered what she thought of him.

He was a few months short of his fortieth birthday.

'You're as old as you feel,' he muttered as he did an about-turn and went into the bathroom. 'And I refuse to feel old.'

Will opened a new packet of disposable razors and squirted shaving foam onto his palm. After he washed his whiskerless face he patted his cheeks with the expensive cologne he'd bought on impulse the previous week, and dragged a comb though his still-damp hair. The reflection staring back at him from the mirror made him grimace. The hair was too much. It made him look like a pomaded Mafia boss. He rearranged his dark mane into its usual state of untidiness with his fingers.

'That's better,' he muttered, but he knew some subtle shift in his thought processes had occurred and he wasn't sure whether to be alarmed or pleased. The adrenaline he usually channelled into his work had taken a different direction and he found these strange thoughts he was having and his peculiar behaviour oddly exhilarating.

He made a snap decision to visit the city shops—something he hadn't done for years.

His expedition took up most of the afternoon. That evening, as he pulled on his trousers, buttoned his shirt and fiddled with his strange new hairstyle, he thought of Sophie's reaction—but it was too late to be having regrets.

She was the reason for it all.

What was done was done and was probably long overdue. He couldn't turn back the clock.

Half an hour later he drove into the car park of the flats where Sophie lived, feeling way out of his comfort zone, but he reminded himself she had only been the catalyst. He had to admit he felt younger, less tired and for the first time in years he experienced a spark of... What? A zest for living? New-found energy? The desire to look good to impress a woman?

And there was no doubt in his muddled mind who that woman was.

Sophie had no excuse for taking so long deciding what to wear. She only had two choices—her deep burgundy equivalent of the *little black dress* or a more conservative outfit of black flared silk trousers paired with a floaty, swirly, off-the-shoulder top she'd bought that morning.

She stood in front of the mirror for a final inspection, grimacing. She missed her three-times-a-week workouts at the gym and had put on a kilo or two. Prodding the skin of her thigh, she wondered, with alarm, if the slight bulge was the beginning of cellulite. Turning to the side and pulling in her stomach before inspecting her backside, she scowled.

'Too clingy. Too revealing,' she muttered as she smoothed the body-hugging fabric from her midriff to the mid-thigh hemline. 'I'll change into the trousers.'

At that moment there was a knock on the door and Sophie looked at her watch. Surely it wasn't Will already? But it was half past seven—he was right on time. Slipping on her high-heeled sandals, she went to open the door.

She was gob-smacked.

All thoughts of her own appearance evaporated.

It was hard to believe the slickly dressed, tall, dark and handsome hunk was the same man she'd worked alongside for the last three weeks.

He looked gorgeous!

She tried to keep a straight face, but by the look on his face she hadn't been as successful as she'd hoped.

The transformation was hard to believe. He was a picture of casual but sophisticated elegance. He wore sleek black tailored trousers sitting snugly on lean, relaxed hips. His long-sleeved deep blue-green shirt revealed just enough of his perfectly proportioned torso to make any red-blooded woman want to see more, and accentuated his naturally olive skin. He was clean shaven with the hint of a sexy five-o'clock shadow.

And his hair… It had been cut fashionably short and professionally styled to look ruffled. The deep brown, almost black colour was natural, but caught the light in a way that glinted with an almost silver sheen.

He surprised her by grinning and doing a self-conscious twirl. The look on his face was apologetic—embarrassed, even.

'Like it?'

What did he expect her to say? That he could come and decorate her living room any day he liked?

'Not bad. A definite improvement.' She chuckled.

He laughed as well, but gave the impression he wasn't completely comfortable with his new look.

'I'll take that as a compliment,' he said with a lingering, hesitant smile. 'And don't *you* look stunning?'

She felt his gaze drift from her hair all the way to her toes and suddenly remembered her dress—the deep V of the neckline that exposed way too much cleavage, the too-short skirt and the clinging fabric revealing bulges she hadn't realised she had.

He was staring at her.

She definitely had to change.

'Can I come in?' he said.

'Yes, sorry—of course.'

'Just sit down while I get changed. I won't be a minute.'

'Get changed? Why? You look fabulous.'

'Are you sure? The dress isn't too...er...?'

'It's perfect, Sophie.' He grinned. 'As long as you can cope with the admiration of all the men present.'

He was almost flirting, but not quite. And she liked it. If Will approved, she'd stay with the dress. It was stretch fabric and would probably...stretch.

'Let's go, then,' she said as she grabbed her purse and linked her arm in his.

Will knew that every pair of eyes at the party, including the women's, would be on Sophie. She was dressed to kill.

He felt protective of her, though, despite the fact he couldn't lay claim to being anything more than her employer and friend providing the courtesy of accompanying her to a party where all the guests would be strangers.

What if she were his date?

He dismissed the thought, realising it was futile to even imagine the possibility of crash-landing in paradise.

They walked the short distance to Andrew's house, weaving their way through the cars belonging to guests who had already arrived—a BMW convertible, a late-model Range Rover and a vintage Porsche. It was like cruising the showroom at Perth's major dealer in luxury cars.

'Specialists must earn good money here,' Sophie said as they reached the elaborate covered entry to Andrew's house.

'The ones Andrew fraternises with do.' He tried to keep the

sarcasm out of his voice. These days Will was rarely invited to functions like this and he had a good idea why.

'The Porsche belongs to Sam Baxter, an extremely popular and successful plastic surgeon who specialises in cosmetic surgery,' he added. 'His wife runs a skin clinic that does dermabrasion, Botox, laser treatment and the like. Exceptionally lucrative and dependent on full-paying private patients. I'm not sure who owns the other cars.'

Sophie didn't reply and appeared to be absorbing the information. She'd feel quite at home with Andrew's guests, he was certain. He pressed the buzzer and a few seconds later the door was opened by a middle-aged man in a dark suit. He promptly took the drinks and seemed to know who they were without introduction.

'Dr Brent, Dr Carmichael, please follow me,' he said formally.

Will glanced at Sophie as they both followed the man into a large, tastefully furnished living room. Andrew broke away from an earnest conversation with Lance Braithwell, a fellow cardiologist. Their host extended his hand to Will and kissed Sophie lightly on the cheek.

'Fabulous you both could come.' His gaze fixed on Sophie, swinging from her dress and its delectable contents back to her face. 'You look absolutely gorgeous, Sophie. Come and meet the other guests.' His hand, the one not holding a bright blue cocktail, found its way to the small of her back as he guided her towards the Baxters. 'What would you like to drink?'

Will took the opportunity to slip away, find the kitchen, and organise his own drink. He felt sure Sophie and her admirers wouldn't miss him.

The kitchen was a hive of activity, and Will was barely noticed as he scanned the contents of a huge fridge dedicated purely to liquid refreshment. He finally found what he was looking for—a particular brand of dry ginger ale which, in the right glass, could pass as light ale. He'd devised various strategies over the years to avoid drawing attention to the fact he was a teetotaller, or the reason why. He always kept a small amount of wine and beer at home for visitors but had never been tempted to imbibe.

He totally understood Sophie's distrust of drinkers and their sometimes irresponsible behaviour. He had no intention of re-visiting a time in his life that had nearly been his undoing by revealing a part of his past he'd rather forget. It was best Sophie didn't know.

Ignoring the questioning look from the teenager washing dishes, he selected a heavy-based beer glass from a crate near the sink and filled it close to the brim. Task accomplished, he made his way back to the party and was content, at least initially, to stand quietly in the background observing, before embracing the task of fundraising.

Not surprisingly, Sophie was sitting on a couch, talking animatedly to an admiring audience of three men, including Andrew, and she gave the impression she was quite capable of looking after herself.

'You must be Will Brent.' A young woman with a tangle of blonde hair, wearing a sleeveless denim mini-dress in the un-likely colour of purple, metallic black ankle boots and a jumble of silver jewellery, sidled up to him. She looked as if she'd be more at home at a rock concert. She'd startled him out of his reverie and he came close to spilling his drink.

'That's right. I don't think I've met you before. You are…?'

'Angie Baxter.' She smiled mischievously. 'Doctor, daughter of Sam and Olivia, recently appointed registrar to Andrew.'

It was difficult for Will to hold back his surprise and she must have picked up on it.

'Surprised? That such conservative parents could produce—?'

His laughter cut her sentence short.

'A little. You don't exactly fit the mould of Andrew's usual guests.'

'Neither do you, or so I've heard.'

'And do you believe what you've heard?'

'Now I've met you…definitely not. In fact, you scrub up nicely for someone who's supposed to hang out on the wrong side of the tracks and work so hard he's forgotten how to have fun.'

Just then Sophie appeared, and for a reason totally unknown to him Will suppressed the sudden urge to explain or apologise or both, as if she were his date.

'Who's forgotten how to have fun?' Sophie said innocently.

'Excuse me.' Angie seemed to lose interest in Will. 'There's something I need to see Andrew about, now he's free. Hope you don't mind?'

'No, of course not,' Will assured her, with a little more enthusiasm than he'd planned.

Sophie stared at him with a quizzical twinkle in her eye.

'I hope I didn't interrupt something important.'

Will shrugged. Sophie was teasing and he liked it. It implied familiarity and being comfortable in the other person's company. He dropped his voice and leaned close.

'I actually found her a bit scary. Would you believe she's Andrew's registrar and…her mother and father are here!'

Sophie laughed. 'No, it wouldn't surprise me at all. Are the Baxters her parents?'

'That's right. How did you guess?'

'They're slightly…how can I put it?…bizarre as well. Olivia's just offered me a cushy job in cosmetic medicine. No interview, no CV or references required. Sam said I qualified for the job on the basis of my looks alone—as an advertisement for their treatments. I wouldn't trust him as far as… Well, I just wouldn't trust him.'

The lightness of Will's mood suddenly took a dive as he began to understand his colleague's motives in wining and dining Sophie Carmichael. She was probably seen as a desirable and youthful addition to the social set Andrew and his cronies moved in. Not only was she decorative and charismatic, but also clever, and the type of graduate who would jump at the chance of a well-paid, relatively undemanding job at such an early stage of her career—particularly if she wanted to marry and have children. That type of long-term job in Western Australia would also solve her problem of getting away from her ex.

'What did you tell him?' Will guessed Sophie had refused the offer, but also hoped she hadn't offended the couple. He'd planned to ask them for either a hefty donation or ongoing sponsorship for the community centre upgrade and he wanted them onside.

'I just thanked them politely and told them I couldn't make any commitments at the moment because I didn't know how long I would be staying in Perth.'

Will smiled, surprised at the intensity of relief he felt. 'Full points for diplomacy,' he said, hiding his emotion, something he was expert at.

'Oh, and of course I mentioned our fundraising, gave the cause a bit of a plug, and they seemed interested. Said they'd be keen to hear what you had planned.'

'That's fabulous.'

He felt like scooping her into his arms and thanking her properly...thoroughly...with a heartfelt kiss, but...

A young man Will hadn't met, who'd recently joined Andrew's private practice as a partner, introduced himself and spirited Sophie away to meet his wife. Will took the opportunity to put on his most charismatic face to work the room, and before he had a chance to catch up with Sophie again the butler appeared, ringing a tiny bell, and announced that dinner was served.

By the end of the main course Sophie had had enough. Her permanent smile made her face ache, she was fed up with the never-ending stream of doctor and lawyer jokes, and she could no longer keep up the façade that she was enjoying herself.

Everyone drank more as the evening progressed.

Except Will. He seemed to make the same glass of beer last all night and contributed very little.

The other guests were letting their hair down, getting louder and cruder, and when the conversation degenerated into cruel criticism of those who weren't there to defend themselves she decided she would make her excuses to leave at the first opportunity.

Also, the tone of the evening as it progressed made her feel edgy—particularly as it looked as if they were all going to drive home.

She wanted to leave. With Will.

Somehow she had been persuaded to sit between Lance Braithwell, recently divorced, and Andrew, perennial playboy. She didn't know how to escape. Will was at the other end of the table, tolerating what appeared to be an endless, one-sided conversation with Angie Baxter. He looked as if he'd reached his limits as well, but she had no idea how to join forces with him and tactfully make an exit.

Finally she had her chance when it was announced that dessert, coffee and liqueurs were being served by the pool and the party moved outside. She approached Will.

'Enjoying yourself?' she asked with what she hoped was tact.

Will shrugged. 'Are you?'

'Not really.' She leaned close and whispered, 'They're boring, Will. They've had too much to drink. I think if I left at this stage of the evening they wouldn't even notice.'

Will responded to her frank assessment with a hoot of laughter.

'Well said. You're absolutely right.' He grasped her hand, moved back from the pool into the shadows and began to walk purposefully towards the side gate. 'I'm game if you are,' he added, with a mischievous grin on his face.

They were both breathless as Will furtively closed the gate. Then Sophie began to giggle. Her mood was contagious as Will tried to muffle his laughter.

'Shush,' Sophie whispered. 'They might send a search party.'

Will grasped her hand and they jogged down Andrew

Fletcher's driveway as fast as Sophie's high heels would allow. A few minutes later they stumbled up the single low step to Sophie's flat and stopped a moment to catch their breath. Will released his grip on Sophie's hand and stood hesitantly.

'Well...' he finally said. 'I guess I'd better get going.'

Sophie could barely see Will's expression in the dim light but his body language suggested disappointment. It was only ten-thirty—hours before Sophie's usual Saturday-night bedtime—and she wasn't ready for her first night out in Perth to finish so soon. She didn't want the evening to end, and deep down she knew it was because she wanted to spend more time Will.

She assumed, from his inability to let go and have a good time, the dinner party had been an ordeal for him. He definitely wasn't comfortable with Andrew's crowd, and she suspected the evening had been purely a means to an end—a way to take his dream a step closer to reality.

Her eyes became accustomed to the gloom and she noticed Will was hovering, as reluctant to part as she was.

She had nothing to lose.

'It's too early, don't you think?'

Sophie was aware of Will tensing and she wondered why. Had she misread his body language? She paused, waiting for his reaction, but he stood motionless in the half-dark.

'I'm not sure what you mean,' he finally said.

'It seems a shame to waste the new clothes, the whole new look by having an early night.' She smiled and reclaimed his hand. 'And I feel I need an antidote to the after-effects of spending several boring hours in the company of Sir Andrew and his friends.'

He laughed. Her attempt at humour worked.

'Great.' His eyes seemed to twinkle in anticipation. 'I'm a bit out of touch with the late-night scene, though.'

'All the more exciting. We'll both be venturing into the unknown.'

'Okay, let's find ourselves somewhere to party.'

As they walked hand in hand to Will's car, Sophie felt a sense of freedom, as if the shackles that bound her to the past had been broken.

The reason was the man beside her.

But she didn't dare think of the future.

CHAPTER NINE

SOPHIE'S suggestion took Will totally by surprise. He wondered if she'd homed in on his reluctance to say goodnight.

But where could he take her? It had been longer then he'd like to admit since he'd set foot in a late-night bar or club, but he didn't want to appear completely out of touch.

'Where would you like to go? Somewhere quiet? I remember a piano bar in one of the old pubs in the city.' He paused to take a breath. He could hardly believe what he was about to say. 'Or perhaps you'd prefer some real excitement. A nightclub, maybe?'

He held his breath and prepared himself for Sophie's laughter but her answer was deadly serious.

'After Andrew, clubbing sounds good to me.'

'Oh.' He felt a tingle of combined exhilaration and trepidation travel from the base of his skull all the way down his spine. Late-night revelling was probably second nature to Sophie and her sophisticated Sydney set. He didn't want to disappoint her.

Did he know any decent nightclubs?

The only one that came to mind was The Quarterdeck. Andrew had invited him to celebrate one of his divorces there a few years back, but Will had politely declined. He remembered, though, that his colleague had said it catered to an older and more sophisticated clientele than the usual night spots.

Sophie was still standing on her doorstep, looking at him expectantly and waiting for a reply.

'You're serious, then?'

'Absolutely.' She was challenging him, probably thinking *fun* was a word that had disappeared from his vocabulary. And she was right.

But he *so* wanted to spend more time with her. And if risking making a total fool of himself was the only way to do it…

'I've heard there's a place in Fremantle that's okay.'

'In the port city?'

'That's right. It's called The Quarterdeck.'

'Sounds good to me. Are you okay to drive?'

Will understood Sophie's concern, but wasn't going to explain he'd been drinking a soft drink.

'I'll be fine. I've only had one all evening,' he said.

She seemed satisfied with that and smiled.

'Shall we go, then?'

There was an undercurrent of tension buzzing in the air as Will drove the ten kilometres to central Fremantle. Was he nervous about spending the rest of the evening with her? Had she put their professional relationship at risk? Comfort-zone boundaries were being stretched again, Sophie thought as Will expertly eased his car into a narrow space about a block away from the nightclub.

'Ready to party?' Will said with a smile that looked a little forced, and Sophie wondered if he was having second thoughts.

'That's what we're here for.'

He made his way around to the passenger side of the car and opened the door for her while she quickly checked her make-up and dragged a comb through her tussled hair.

'You look gorgeous,' Will said, appearing slightly embarrassed.

He locked his car and then took her hand. She could easily get used to cradling this man's warm strong fingers in hers. It felt right, somehow.

'It's this way,' he added.

They walked the length of the narrow side street in silence and then turned into the main road, which bustled with activity. Crowded bars spilled their patrons onto open-air drinking areas. Late-night diners filled the many restaurants and a queue of about twenty people snaked its way towards the entrance of The Quarterdeck. Sophie sighed with relief when she saw that most of the patrons were in their late twenties and thirties—a mixture of couples, groups and singles.

'Do you think the queue means we have to wait for people to come out before we can go in?' Will asked as they took their place at its tail.

'I doubt it. It's still early and unlikely that the place is full.'

Will laughed. 'You call eleven o'clock early? I'm usually tucked up in bed by now.'

Sophie sent him a sideways glance.

'Lucky you.' Her tone was light, the words easily taking on a double meaning, but she didn't have a chance to gauge Will's reaction. The line moved forward as a large group at the front gained entry and it wasn't long before the entrance fee was paid in exchange for the mark of a small rubber stamp on the backs of their hands and admission to a loud, hot, pulsating den of night-life.

Sophie felt energised.

Will looked bewildered.

'Come on!' she shouted. 'Over there—near the bar. There's a table free. You'd like a drink before we dance, wouldn't you?'

Will nodded mutely and didn't complain as she led him across a dance floor crammed with a seething mass of people.

'Let me buy you a drink.'

'No, I—'

'Just the first one, to thank you for bringing me out to rage. It's the least I—'

But her voice was drowned out by the music and he seemed so overwhelmed he was beyond protest.

She'd have to get something special, she thought, and decided at that moment she would be skipper for the night. If he wanted a drink or two on what she presumed was his first Saturday night out for…well…probably longer than she could even guess, he wouldn't have to worry about driving.

Shouldering her way through to the bar, she scrutinised the cocktail list and found the one she wanted—the one she'd been introduced to by her best friend Anna on the night of her last final-year exam.

'What's in your All Night Long?' she requested when she finally caught the attention of one of the bar staff.

The barman listed the familiar ingredients.

'And pineapple juice?'

'That's the one, darling. With a dash of lemon and lime.' The brawny bartender winked. 'You want one?'

'Yes, and a pineapple juice in the same type of glass, thanks.'

After he'd carefully measured and mixed the drink, Sophie couldn't help taking a sip of the delectable cocktail she'd bought for Will, hoping he'd accept it in good spirits. It was just as she remembered—the perfect combination of smoothness and bite, designed to be sipped slowly, every drop savoured.

She glanced across to where Will sat and smiled. He was vigorously shaking his head at three young women who were vying for his attention and the seat he seemed to be guarding jealously—presumably for her. Always the gentleman.

He looked relieved when she arrived back at the table and the women left them in peace.

'That looks fancy.' Will grinned as she placed the drinks on the table.

'My favourite special-occasion drink.'

'Special occasion?' The music began again after a short break and Will leaned close to her so he could be heard. His breath was warm on her cheek and she could tell he was becoming swept up in the heady, effervescent mood of the place. His cheeks were slightly flushed and one leg began to move with the throbbing rhythm of the music. Sophie anticipated little persuasion would be needed to get him up to dance.

'My first night out in a new city.' She'd almost said *first date*, but checked herself just in time. It was ludicrous to even contemplate them being a couple.

'And *my* first night out for longer than I can remember.' Will stirred his drink with the bright plastic swizzle stick, its top shaped like an anchor, and took a sip. To her dismay, he frowned. 'What's in it?'

'That's a secret between me and the barman. Don't you like it?'

'It's not that.' He hesitated. 'I don't drink…when I'm driving.'

'I'll drive,' she said with a smile, and pointed to her drink. 'Just pineapple juice.'

'We can swap, then.'

He moved the glasses with a determination that showed he wasn't going to argue, and Sophie suddenly remembered what her father had told her—what she'd dismissed as manipulative and misguided gossip.

Maybe Will didn't touch alcohol at all. Other than at Andrew's, where his one drink had seemed to last for ever, she'd never seen him have an alcoholic drink. In fact, she hadn't seen him pour his drink at the dinner party and couldn't be absolutely sure what it was. Perhaps she'd have the courage to ask him later.

By that time the volume of the music made conversation near impossible and they were both content to watch the rabble of clubbers, Will in apparent wide-eyed wonder. She was enjoying herself more than she had in a long time. It felt so good to be out having uncomplicated fun with a man she liked and knew she could trust. It was easy just being with Will.

Swept up in the moment she stood and grasped his hand.

'Come on, let's dance.'

Will grinned and downed the last two mouthfuls of his drink.

'You don't know what you're letting yourself in for,' he shouted.

'Let me be the judge of that.' Sophie doubted he heard her reply.

They managed to blend in with the roiling mob, but despite the crowd around her Sophie's awareness suddenly focused. Her partner, gradually shedding his inhibitions, grabbed one of her hands and swung her in an intimate arc until their bodies collided with reckless anticipation. It was as if she and Will had the dance floor to themselves. He pulled her towards him, his pelvis pressed hard into her belly and his hips swaying to the primal pulse of the music.

His lips grazed her forehead and left her skin smarting and her body confused. He inclined his head and said in a rasping whisper, 'I'll stop if—'

'No, don't stop.'

It was probably no more than ten minutes that Sophie and Will spent locked in an abandoned embrace, oblivious to anything other than the music and themselves, but for Sophie it felt like a lifetime.

She didn't want it to end.

Her awareness of every muscle of Will's body, the firm pressure of one hand in the small of her back and the other sliding seductively from just below her shoulder blade to her backside and back and his warm, uneven breath touching her forehead had every nerve ending painfully primed for pleasure.

She wanted him.

If it was purely lust, she didn't care.

If this extraordinarily sexy man was willing, what was the harm? If they both had a physical need, an infuriating itch that desperately needed scratching, then why not?

Rules were made to be broken.

When the music stopped she had no doubt he was just as aroused as she was, and when he said, 'Shall we go?' Sophie knew he wasn't asking because he was bored or disenchanted with the club. He wanted to be alone with her.

He wanted *her.*

She answered, 'Yes,' without hesitation, and didn't know how long she could wait.

They were both breathless as they walked towards the corner of the street where Will's car was parked, but there was no doubt in his mind—Will knew what he was doing. Although the music, the dancing and the mesmerising feeling of being part of a like-minded crowd had loosened him up, his head was clear. He'd even given himself time to think through what had happened on the dance floor.

It was a wonderful, magical but purely physical desire he felt for Sophie. The unfamiliar set of circumstances—the atmosphere, the noise, the combined raw energy of the patrons in the club—had triggered a bubbling to the surface of something he'd kept inside too long.

His sexuality.

He'd just had no need for it, and he'd viewed it as a hindrance to the things he considered important in his life.

But now...having kissed Sophie on an impulse a fortnight ago, having been so close to making love to her on the dance floor...he knew the urge was more powerful than mere reasoned restraint.

And Sophie was hot—there was no other word for it.

The experience was invigorating, all-consuming and tantalisingly acute. He didn't need to waste words on asking Sophie how she felt or what she wanted either.

He knew.

They rounded the corner, and now they were away from prying eyes he needed at least to kiss her.

He pinned her against the rough brick wall and she groaned.

'I hold you responsible,' she said, with the barest hint of a smile.

'Full responsibility accepted.'

The words were barely out of his mouth before his lips found hers. Her mouth was delicious. She tasted of fruit, a hint of coffee, and something he could only describe as sexy and very feminine.

Her hands were on the back of his head, steadying, possessing and ensuring the captured kiss lasted as long as *she* wanted.

And it lasted. Long and lingering.

She pressed her mouth hard against his and then bit his lower lip before opening up to him. Their mutual exploration left him gasping as he realised his whole body was responding.

And Sophie knew it.

Her lips still caressed as she pressed one teasing thigh between his legs while her other leg somehow tangled around his knee, almost straddling him, exciting him beyond endurance.

She pulled away and opened her eyes, a startled look on her face.

'Not here,' she whispered.

'No.' He caught his breath, slightly embarrassed that he'd become so immersed in the moment he'd lost sight of where they were.

'Come back to my place,' Sophie said, her voice laced with the same urgency *he* was feeling. 'It's closer,' she added with a cheeky smile that drizzled into his being like melted chocolate. He had no objections.

'Okay.'

The word was barely out of his mouth when a skinny, scantily clad girl of about sixteen or seventeen emerged from a lane-way twenty metres or so from where they stood. She looked stoned and desperate, and Will found himself alert—primed for danger. He'd be surprised if she was on her own, and a number of scenarios went through his head.

He had no problem if she turned out to be simply a passer-by or genuinely needed help but, with his experience of how some of the teenagers in Prevely Springs managed to survive, he had to be sure.

Sophie was busy adjusting her dress and hadn't noticed. She looked up as the girl began to stumble towards them, crying. Then Sophie moved so fast Will didn't have a chance to stop her.

Sophie wondered why Will hesitated when the girl was obviously distressed and needed help. It was instinct to go to her and find out what was wrong.

'What's the matter?'

The teenager's tears turned to sobs. 'I… My friend…'

Sophie grasped the girl's shoulders. She made no sense.

'What's your name?'

She stopped sobbing and took a ragged intake of breath.

'Emma.'

Sophie felt a firm hand on her own shoulder and turned to see Will with a look of disapproval on his face.

'What's she told you?' he asked.

'Nothing yet. Just her name.'

Emma was shaking now, her skin mottled despite the mildness of the night.

Sophie ignored Will and moved towards the teenager, putting her arm around her shoulders and confirming she was cold.

'We can't help you if you don't tell us what's wrong, Emma.'

'Be careful, Sophie.'

She glanced briefly at Will but continued. 'Your friend? Is there something wrong with your friend?'

'We took some stuff. The guy said it was like speed but better because it'd make us feel good without the aggro. We'd chill out and relax.'

Sophie began walking towards the lane-way, aware of Will at her heel.

'What happened then?'

'Everything was cool, but then my friend Lexie, she was sick, and had some kind of fit. The guy, he just ran, left us, and I can't get Lex to wake up.' She began sobbing again. 'You've got to help us. She mustn't die.'

'Okay, where is Lexie? Can you show us?'

It was the first sign from Will that he was prepared to help. He leaned towards Sophie and spoke quietly, as if he didn't want Emma to hear.

'Let me go first. You stay back—just until we make sure it's safe.'

'What?' Sophie didn't understand why he wouldn't believe the girl. Anyone could tell she was scared witless.

'Just trust me on this one. I've been in the same place as Emma. I know how her world works and it's not always kind.'

Sophie dropped back as they followed Emma into the lane. They were only a few metres in when they saw the other teenager slumped against a skip bin.

Will started to run.

'She doesn't look good,' he called as he reached the girl, who appeared to be unconscious.

Sophie wasn't far behind.

Will checked she was breathing then laid her on her side. He inspected her pupils—not easy in the dim light—and barked an instruction to Sophie.

'Ring for an ambulance. Tell them we've got an unconscious teenager with a probable drug overdose and it looks like she has some respiratory depression. Do you know the name of the street?'

Emma's frightened form emerged from the shadows. 'Genevieve Lane, off Alcott Street.'

'Good girl.' Will's tone was reassuring and Emma managed a smile.

Sophie reached the emergency services on her mobile phone and was connected to the ambulance base communications officer. She relayed what she knew, and added that although there were two doctors in attendance they had no equipment and could only administer at-the-scene first aid. She made it quite clear it was a life-or-death emergency.

Lexie was lucky. There was a large tertiary hospital nearby, and an ambulance was promised in five to ten minutes. Her chances of survival and recovery were good, even if she stopped breathing and needed CPR before the paramedics arrived.

'Five minutes.' Sophie relayed the information to Will, whose fingers were on Lexie's neck, feeling for her pulse.

'Good. The sooner, the better.' Will directed his gaze at Emma. 'You did the right thing. I think she'll be okay.'

Sophie saw some of Emma's anxiety dissipate and was glad Will's sensitivity had returned.

'Can you wait for the ambulance at the entrance to the lane to show them where we are?' he added.

Emma shuffled back to the street.

'You really think she'll be okay?' Sophie asked, sensing there was nothing more that Will could do other than maintain the girl's airway and monitor the vital signs he was able to measure without equipment.

He took his eyes off his patient and looked at Sophie long enough for her to see that his expression was one of unfathomable pain. She knew now was not the time to ask why.

'I think so. It's possible she's a street kid, but I don't think she's on hard drugs. More likely a one-off dose of a party drug. They're often contaminated. Her history—the short time between euphoria and then vomiting and convulsions before she passed out—suggests it might be GHB.'

'No reversal drug?'

'No, the opiate antidote has no effect but we always give it. You have little to lose in a comatose patient, but if they've been using narcotics it can mean the difference between life and death. A good proportion of heroin ODs are resuscitated at the scene and don't even need hospitalisation.'

'I've heard they often refuse to go to hospital when they wake up.'

'Right, and you rarely get any thanks.'

Sophie felt the bitterness in Will's words but had no time for reflection on her colleague's attitude to drug-users.

They heard the ambulance siren gradually getting closer, and Emma waved frantically from the pavement at the end of the lane.

'They're here,' she shouted, as the bright green and white vehicle pulled up. The driver stopped briefly to talk to Emma and then slowly reversed down the lane.

A briskly efficient woman jumped from the passenger seat, gathering her resuscitation kit. Her colleague followed with a stretcher, an oxygen cylinder and another large bag.

'I'm Liz. What have we got here?' She leaned over the girl, looking and feeling for respiration, slipping an airway into Lexie's mouth, feeling her pulse, checking her pupils.

'Took an unknown oral drug. Her friend said she started vomiting, then fitted and finally lost consciousness.'

She glanced at Sophie. 'And you're both doctors?'

'Mmm.'

'Looks like it was this kid's lucky night, then. What do you think she took?' She was addressing Will now.

'I'm not positive, but my first guess from the history and the fact she's unusually cold, has a bradycardia, respiratory depression and is out of it—'

'GHB?'

'Right.'

'Second callout tonight.' Liz's partner spoke as he was preparing to insert an IV line.

'That's Geoff.'

He nodded while positioning the cannula into one of the fragile veins in Lexie's forearm.

'He was about the same age but in much worse shape. Had to be intubated.' He taped in the tube, connected the bag of fluid and then drew medication from an ampoule, which his partner checked.

'We'll give naloxone here, though, and if there's no response she'll need to go to the ED. Do you think she's likely to arrest?' Liz asked.

'She's been unconscious but stable since we've been here—about ten minutes—with no deterioration in her resps.'

Will threw a glance in Sophie's direction. She felt redundant.

'Do you want me to go in the ambulance?' He'd directed the question to the paramedics.

'No, there's no need. They're expecting us and it's only five minutes to the hospital. Any response?' Liz asked Geoff, who was carefully giving increments of the antidote drug at one-minute intervals. The effect to reverse opiate toxicity was usually rapid—within minutes. Lexie's lack of response suggested she hadn't OD'd on heroin or related drugs.

'Nah, and that's the max—two milligrams. I think it's time to move her out.'

'Can I go with her?' a small voice interrupted.

Sophie suddenly felt guilty about neglecting Emma.

'Of course. The doctors will need your help.' Liz smiled at the girl. 'And when Lexie wakes up, I bet she'll want a hand to hold.'

The two paramedics with all their paraphernalia wheeled Lexie the short distance to the ambulance.

'Thanks for your help,' Geoff called.

As Liz passed Sophie, she said quietly with a wink, 'Enjoy the rest of the evening. Lucky you. He's gorgeous.'

CHAPTER TEN

THE magic of that breathless, heady encounter, when Will had pressed Sophie's willing body up against the wall and kissed her, had dissolved as soon as Emma had staggered from the lane-way. By the look on Will's face it was unlikely to be recaptured—that night, at least.

'She should be okay,' Will said, as if he was talking to a colleague after a successful resuscitation.

'What will they do at the hospital?'

'If she shows no signs of deterioration she'll most likely be admitted for monitoring and observation. Although she didn't improve before the ambulance arrived, the kid stayed stable, so I doubt she'll get worse.'

'That's good.'

'And they'll do toxicology, of course.'

'Mmm.' Sophie had seen enough kids with drug habits to know resuscitation from an OD was only the tip of the iceberg. 'Will she be followed up?'

Will turned and looked at her with sadness in his eyes.

'Appointments are made, but you're lucky to get fifty per cent to show up. The biggest problem is trying to break the cycle.'

Sophie knew what he meant. Treating the effects of drugs didn't address the cause—the set of circumstances that had led to young person's substance abuse in the first place.

'The youth centre should make a big difference.'

Will slowed his walking pace a little and looked directly into Sophie's eyes. His weekday weariness had returned.

'Before you came on board I was beginning to wonder if it would ever get off the ground.' He sighed. 'I thought the process would be easy but I still feel I'm fighting an uphill battle.'

Will still gave the impression he was shouldering the whole load and Sophie wanted to let him know he was no longer alone.

'But we're trying to get the people of the Springs involved. The folk who will benefit. The centre will have more meaning if they've actually helped to make it happen.'

'That's not been the major problem.' A hint of a smile brightened his gloomy expression. 'Grass-roots support doesn't make any difference to how slowly the bureaucratic wheels turn.'

Sophie couldn't think of anything reassuring to say, so she stayed silent and her thoughts returned to the two teenagers they'd helped. Emma had seemed a caring kid, at least, and Sophie had the feeling the girls weren't addicts—she hoped they had just been experimenting and had the sense to learn from the night's experience. The type of centre Will was working so hard to set up would be ideal to follow up kids like Emma and Lexie—to try and keep them on track, to break the cycle of cause and effect.

Will and Sophie had been walking and talking and were now only a few metres from Will's car. Sophie was disappointed that Will was so distant. He hadn't even offered to hold her hand. Perhaps what had buzzed between them a short time ago had been illusory—purely a result of the near frenzied atmosphere of the club and their mutual loneliness.

Not reason enough to jump into bed together.

Will opened the car door for her.

'Thanks.' Sophie smiled but Will's face was impassive.

'I'll drop you home.' It was a statement from Will, not a question.

They travelled the entire journey to Sabiston in silence, and when they arrived at Sophie's flat she was wide awake. She knew it would take time for her to relax enough to sleep. She craved company, Will's company.

'Do you want to come in—?'

'No, I—'

From the look on his face he'd misunderstood.

Sophie smiled. 'Just for a coffee. I'm a bit wound up after what happened and could do with the company…just to talk.'

He grinned sheepishly.

'Yes, I'd like that.' He paused and took longer than he needed to turn the engine off and extract the key from the ignition. He glanced briefly in her direction but seemed embarrassed. 'What happened between us...'

He wanted out.

'Impulsive—in the heat of the moment.'

'A mistake.'

Not in Sophie's view, but they both needed time to reassess the consequences of a short affair with no possibility of a future. From what she'd gleaned of Will's personality in the short time they'd known each other, he wouldn't embark on anything without giving one hundred per cent.

'Right,' she lied, but knew it was for the best.

They got out of the car and made their way to the flat in the light of the dim car-park lamps. The soft yellowish glow cast shadows and a light breeze stirred leaf litter from the single plane tree behind the flats—the only sound, other than their footsteps, to disturb the clear, moonlit night. The atmosphere created was eerily sensual and Will looked particularly handsome with his shadowed jaw, ruffled clothes and uncertain expression.

Sophie wondered if she'd made a mistake by inviting Will in when she had the sudden urge to reassure him by putting her arms around his beautiful body and just holding him. He seemed so vulnerable and alone.

She turned on the light.

'Come in, Will. Make yourself at home,' she managed as she regained her composure.

Sophie looked around the small living-dining room and wished the furnishings were less sparse. The single sofa and the modest two-place dining setting provided the only seating, and she needed to maintain some distance from Will.

'Sit down.' Sophie made a sweeping gesture, leaving Will to make the decision of where to sit, suddenly wondering why it mattered so much. 'I'll make coffee. Okay?'

'Great.' He pulled out one of the chairs from the table and sat where he could watch her prepare the drinks. 'Need any help?'

'No, thanks.'

It was polite small talk. Sophie relaxed as she added water to the kettle and coffee to the plunger.

'You've settled in, then?'

'Yes. The flat's great. There's a park a block away, a supermarket nearby. I've even had a cup of tea with my elderly next-door neighbours.'

Sophie brought a tray with mugs, coffee-maker, milk and sugar to the table. She poured Will's drink the way she remembered he liked it—black and strong—then nudged the sugar in his direction as she sat opposite him.

'Okay?'

'Fine.' He stirred a generous spoonful of sugar into his cup and then absently added another. He looked up at her. 'Have you managed to get any spare time since you've been here...to enjoy yourself?' He chuckled but it sounded unnatural, contrived even. 'Done any sightseeing?'

'No sightseeing. I've done some shopping, and I swam a few laps in the pool at the local gym this morning.'

'Good.' He looked as if his mind was somewhere else and they both sipped their drinks in silence for a very long minute or two before it began to feel uncomfortable. As Will adjusted the cuff of one sleeve and began fiddling with the button on the other cuff Sophie recalled something Will had said when he'd attended to Lexie. It had played on her mind at the time.

'Do you mind if I ask you something personal?'

He looked at her, initially with slight irritation, before he rearranged his face and laughed.

'My personal life is as boring as mud. Fire away.'

Sophie boldly continued, despite his dismissal.

'You said you'd been in the same place as Lexie.' The smile froze on his face. 'What did you mean?'

He looked away, as if gazing through the window at something in the distance, but the only view was the early-morning dark. Sophie assumed he was thinking, deciding if he trusted her enough to give her an honest answer.

'It's a long story.' He focused back on Sophie and locked her eyes in a frighteningly intense look. 'How much time have you got?'

She was wide awake and had all night. Neither of them had to work the following day.

'As long as it takes.'

Was he about to close off from her? Or had he decided to reveal a secret he guarded as if it was a curse?

Their coffee was going cold. Sophie felt like something stronger.

'I've got a bottle of Chardonnay in the fridge. Would you share it with me?'

He didn't hesitate.

'No, thanks. I don't drink—'

'And drive.' She finished the sentence, remembering what he'd told her in the club and still dismissing her father's revelations about Will's past.

'Do you mind if I have one?'

'Of course not.'

Will stood, scraping the chair awkwardly on the hard floor but not seeming to mind. He collected the half-empty cups and put them on the tray.

'I think I overdid the sugar,' he said with a grimace. 'I'll get the wine. You go and sit on the couch and make yourself comfortable.'

'You sure? I can—'

'Don't worry. I think I know where everything is.' He'd already opened the fridge and found the bottle. He held it up for her to see. 'Wine—fridge; glass—glasses cupboard; corkscrew—knick-knacks drawer,' he said, with just enough cheeky sarcasm to make her laugh.

'Okay, I believe you. You're capable of finding your way around my kitchen.'

She crossed the short distance to the sofa and sat in one corner of the large and comfortable couch, slipped off her sandals and tucked her feet under her bottom. She no longer felt nervous about being physically close to Will and decided she'd go with the flow and let the rest of the evening take its own course.

As Will found the corkscrew and uncorked the wine he tried to decide how much of his past he was prepared to reveal to Sophie. He had no family left who would remember and he'd never told anyone else—not even Tanya. He'd never wanted to. Though his mother's death and his own brief experience with drugs had had a profound influence on the choices he'd made in his life, he didn't like to dwell on the past. He hoped he'd moved on.

There was something about Sophie's gentle probing, though, that demanded an explanation of his behaviour with the teenagers earlier in the evening. He'd reveal whatever he was comfortable with, he decided.

He found a diet cola in the fridge, brought the wine bottle and glasses to the coffee table and poured Sophie's drink. He sat down, angling himself in the corner between the arm and the back of the seat. The couch was roomy enough so they weren't touching. He wasn't quite sure why but it seemed important that there was at least a small physical distance between them.

'So, tell me about yourself.' Her smile was tentative.

'You know a little already.'

'The important stuff?' Sophie sipped her wine.

'Some. You've seen my house. You know it belonged to my grandparents and that they brought me up.'

Sophie didn't prompt him to continue but he could tell she wanted to hear more.

'I can't deny I had a happy childhood. They did the best they could, but June and Albie were getting on in years. June was in her early forties when she had my mum—the miracle baby from God who arrived after so much waiting.'

'And your mother's dead?'

'She abandoned me when I was two and died of an overdose of alcohol and benzodiazepines three years later, when my grandparents thought she'd come off the hard drugs. They were devastated, but I was too young to comprehend.'

It was easier than he'd thought, exposing the naked truth of himself that he'd kept buried in a dark place too long. Sophie put down her drink and reached for his hand. Her steady warmth comforted him.

'My grandparents were completely honest about everything. As soon as I was old enough to understand they told me how my mother had died and that there was no way of knowing who my father was… But they loved me and would do anything for me. That was something they didn't have to tell me, I knew. They seemed to invest everything in me. I was the son they never had. They didn't want to make the same mistakes they'd made with my mother. I was their golden-haired boy. And I let them down.'

'How?' Sophie's voice was a soft whisper and her eyes were moist with the tears *he'd* never been able to shed.

'Can't you guess?'

He knew it was an unfair question, but he needed a moment before he could go on. The telling was a kind of pain that had to happen before he could be set free. How had he not known it before?

Sophie shrugged.

'Drugs? That would explain...'

'Yeah, I guess it explains a lot, but it doesn't make it right.' He took a gulp of his drink, then another.

'I did the predictable teenage thing. Got in with the wrong crowd. Started wasting my life and my grandparents' money on drugs. I spent a year deadening my brain with alcohol and dope before I started on speed.'

'Heroin?'

'No, fortunately I didn't get that far, but on my seventeenth birthday I ended up in hospital, out of my brain on a cocktail of uppers and some prescription antidepressants that one of my so-called mates stole from his mum.'

He took a deep breath. The memories came flooding back as fresh in his mind as if it were yesterday.

'I was lucky I didn't kill myself.' He couldn't help smiling.

'What's funny?' Tears trickled down Sophie's face and his own eyes were moist.

'The irony of it.'

'Irony?'

'I had a deep loathing for the police and it was probably them who saved me.'

Sophie moved closer to Will so her head rested on his shoulder. Her arm entwined in his and she held his hand tight, as if she was afraid of losing him.

'What happened?'

'They were called to the party. I was remorselessly abusive, though I gather not physically aggressive. They took me in via the hospital, because I emptied the contents of my stomach in their van and promptly passed out.

'The doctors in Emergency punished me with two lots of gastric lavage, and I reckon they found the most junior intern and inexperienced nurse to treat me. And I don't blame them. I deserved to have my stomach pumped.'

'Even if you didn't need it?' Sophie was smiling too.

'For sure. A bastard of a tube stuck down my gullet, the

biggest funnel I'd ever seen, and unlimited quantities of fluid being pumped in and out… I tell you, that was a defining moment for me.'

He'd never been able to see any humour in the downward spiral his life had taken in his teen years. It was a liberating experience to laugh at some of the events of so long ago.

'So what happened? You must have finished school to get into medicine and get your degrees.'

It was so easy to tear his heart open for Sophie.

'Albie died. It was only a month after I got into trouble. I blamed myself totally. I believed I'd killed him even though he was eighty-one, had diabetes and ischemic heart disease and was probably a heart attack waiting to happen.'

'And you survived all that?'

'My grandfather was in hospital a week before he died. I stopped taking drugs the day of his heart attack and went in with June every day to visit, sometimes staying so late the night staff booted me out when they started their shift about ten.' He laughed. 'They all thought I was an angel—the perfect grandson.' The slow sigh came from deep within. 'I had lots of time to think—to re-evaluate the reason for my existence and to decide how best I could help my grandparents. June was so proud her grandson was training to become a doctor…' The words stuck in his throat. 'But she didn't live to see me graduate.' Will held back tears. 'She died of a stroke five years after Albie passed away.'

He looked down at Sophie, grasped her chin and tilted her head so he could see her face.

'You must have been highly motivated to study medicine,' Sophie said.

'I had a good brain, so my teachers always said on my school reports, just a bad attitude. So I decided to use my brain, took university entrance subjects at college, gained entry to medicine as a mature student and…' He kissed Sophie's forehead. 'Here I am.'

'Looking after people like your grandparents. Battlers. And kids like the one you used to be.'

'You've got it.'

Sophie brought his hand up to her lips and kissed it lightly. She took a few moments to absorb what he'd said.

'And you've...er...never married?'

Her question stabbed directly into his heart.

'No.' He felt drained and wanted to close the subject, but Sophie persisted. Her intuition had kicked in again.

'Why not?' She rubbed her thumb across the back of his hand and the repetitive action was surprisingly soothing. What did he have to lose?

'I came close. Her name was Tanya. We were both too young. I was in the second year of my medical degree, June had just suffered her first stroke, and I was still weighed down with guilt.' He cleared his throat and swallowed, but it didn't stop the husky emotion in his voice. 'Andrew came along and swept Tanya off her feet.'

Sophie attempted a smile. 'You're a survivor, that's for sure.'

He wasn't about to tell her that had been the second time in his life he nearly *hadn't* survived. He'd used alcohol, not drugs, after Andrew and Tanya had cruelly betrayed him, to numb the pain. A time in his life he'd rather forget.

He hoped Sophie understood now who he was, why he continued to work in a rough neighbourhood notorious for its high level of poverty and crime. If he pulled even one kid out of the gutter and set him on the road to a better life, he felt he'd begin to repay the debt he owed his grandparents.

'So, having my practice in Preverly Springs is my way of paying back my grandparents, Sophie Carmichael.'

'I can see that,' she said softly, and then they both gave up on suppressing enormous yawns.

Will looked at his watch. 'Lord, it's two o'clock. I'd better go.'

Sophie stretched. 'You're overtired and I'd guess emotionally drained.' She patted his hand as they stood. 'Would you like to stay here tonight?'

Of course he would.

But he knew he couldn't. There was too much at stake. Sophie was…like no other woman he'd ever met. Underneath her bubbly, carefree and pampered exterior was a heart so big and kind and loving he could easily fall head over heels for her.

In fact, he was beginning to feel it happening already.

And love… Well, it meant commitment.

The night of lust-driven sex that could easily have happened if they hadn't been interrupted earlier in the evening didn't sit right in his conscience. She deserved better—and he wasn't in the position to provide anything more.

The attraction was there, he had no doubt, but the circumstances were all wrong. It could never work.

He smiled and then kissed her lightly on the cheek, trying his best to give the impression he'd read nothing more into her offer than the provision of spare blankets so he could sleep on the couch.

'Thanks, but, no, thanks.'

Sophie seemed to understand.

'Okay.' She hesitated a moment before wrapping her arms around him and hugging him. Then she stepped back and looked directly into his eyes before continuing.

'I can imagine how hard it must have been…'

He shrugged. The conversation was becoming too intimate. He'd opened his heart to this young woman and shared part of himself that he'd offered to no one else. Now he needed time alone, to try and make some sense out of what to do next.

'I'm fine.' He gathered his keys and they both walked to the door. 'I'll see you Monday.'

The previous evening had been a powerful experience for Will. He'd gone to sleep thinking of Sophie and she was still in his mind when he woke the next morning. Not only had she shown him how to relax and have fun again but she'd rekindled emotions he'd kept buried for half a lifetime.

She'd also awakened sexual feelings he'd kept in check for so long he'd been surprised and a little awed by their ferocity. But the physical awareness hadn't happened overnight. Thinking back, his attraction to Sophie had probably begun the day he'd met her and had been simmering in the background, waiting for the right moment to reach boiling point.

He'd come close after they'd left the club last night. It would have been so easy to succumb…

But now the previous night seemed like a dream. Sophie was easy to be with, easy to work with…easy to love. But she was from a different world. He could tell she missed her young, upwardly mobile friends and the hectic social life she'd left behind. Her suggestion to go out after they'd left Andrew's had most likely been a result of sheer boredom rather than any desire to spend more time with him. He was crazy to think she had feelings for him. Any sort of future together was out of the question.

She had her whole life ahead of her, and was just starting out in her career. She could pick and choose the work she wanted; in fact, she had what some might consider an ideal job waiting for her back in Sydney.

He wondered if *she* realised the full implications of embarking on a personal relationship with him. The medical practice he'd literally saved from the gutter, his patients, the work he did with people mainstream society often rejected was his life. He couldn't move away. Not in the foreseeable future.

If the unlikely happened and she decided to stay on, it had to be for the right reasons. Not staying out of guilt, or pity, or purely because she needed an escape from a difficult period in her life. She was on the rebound and he happened to be the first eligible male she'd bumped into…

He needed his partner in the practice to be as committed as he was.

She seemed to be getting over the break-up with her fiancé,

and she'd have no problem finding new suitors. He didn't know how to live in her world and she would probably tire of him before too long.

They'd had a fun night out together...but that was all. They were totally incompatible for anything more than a one-night stand. He didn't do one-nighters. It was total commitment or nothing for him—in his relationships as well as his work. Maybe he was a perfectionist, setting high goals for himself, but he'd seen the mess his mother had made of her life and there was no way he was going to repeat any of her mistakes. He knew commitment to a life with him wouldn't be easy and she would have to be a very special woman...his Ms Right.

He pulled on faded jeans and shrugged into a crumpled shirt, wondering what he'd done to deserve a life full of so many complications.

He'd just have to stop thinking of his Ms Right...especially in terms of Dr Sophie Carmichael.

CHAPTER ELEVEN

SOPHIE spent most of Sunday trying to clear her mind of thoughts of Will. She cleaned the flat until it gleamed, spent an hour at the pool, caught up with her e-mails and replied to them all—but the thoughts wouldn't go away.

When her phone rang just as she was about to order take-away, she half hoped it was Will.

'Hello?' Sophie recognised her parents' Sydney number and wondered why her father was ringing again. She'd only spoken to him the previous day.

'Darling, how are you?'

She sighed. It wasn't like him to ring her for a friendly chat. She hoped he wasn't about to lecture her yet again on the morals, verified or not, of her boss and the merits of packing her bags and going home.

'I'm fine, Dad.' She cleared her throat, knowing there was a reason for his call, wondering how long it would take for him to travel the circuitous route before he actually told her. 'How are you?'

'Missing you, Sophie, but otherwise excellent.'

'Great.'

Her father coughed, and she imagined him formulating in his mind some request he was going to make or some important news he was about to impart.

'It's wonderful to hear from you, Dad. A pleasant surprise, and I really appreciate your call. Was there anything...?'

'I wondered how you were coping with the work over there. You've been away a while now and I thought you'd have an idea when you were coming home.'

She wouldn't be surprised if he'd been making more enquiries about Will's practice. He'd informed her on his last call that he'd tracked down another couple of doctors who'd worked in the West. He'd already tried to find out about Prevely Springs and appeared to enjoy collecting ammunition to use against her employer. He'd never be happy with the simple truth, though.

'I'm enjoying it, Dad. The practice is very different from home. Most of the patients are low income or on benefits, so their problems can be challenging. But that's what I'm here for—a change and to broaden my experience.'

'What's he like, this Dr William Brent?'

He said each word of Will's name as if he'd been forced to say something particularly unpleasant. Sophie's skin tingled at the thought of telling her father the truth of how she felt about Will. For a start, he didn't hail from Sydney, hadn't been to a private school, and definitely came from the wrong side of the tracks. The cards were stacked against him. She had no doubt her father practised his own kind of snobbery—particularly when it came to the company his oldest daughter kept. And he'd liked Jeremy. Sophie's father hadn't even tried to hide his disappointment when they'd broken up, choosing to ignore the fact her fiancé had been two-timing her.

Will was playing in a totally different field but she didn't expect her father to understand.

'He's dedicated, experienced, hard-working.'

'Has he contacts over there? Are you meeting the right people? Have you managed to catch up with David and Felicity Barr?'

At least he wasn't harping on about Will's alleged drinking problem. Perhaps he'd decided to woo her back home by other means.

'Not yet, Dad. I haven't really had time.'

The last thing she felt like talking about was Andrew

Fletcher's dinner party, knowing her father would approve of his guest list.

'No, of course not.' He paused. Maybe he was finally going to disclose what he'd really phoned about.

'So you'll stick out the next few weeks, you think?'

'Yes.'

'And then you'll be back?'

'Look, Dad, all I can say at the moment is that I plan to stay for the time I've committed to, and then who knows? If things work out I might stay on—'

'For another few weeks?'

'Maybe. I'm not sure yet.'

'Oh, it's just that Janet Willis has dropped a bombshell.'

Janet was a GP about her father's age and had been working at his practice for as long as Sophie could remember. Sophie got on well with her—the only other woman in a male-dominated practice.

'Why? What do you mean?'

Janet was as steady as a rock, dependably calm in a crisis, and took her fair share of the typically demanding, well-heeled female patients who often just needed a sounding board. Sophie's first concern was that she was unwell.

'Is she sick?'

'No, nothing like that. She's leaving us.'

Now Sophie understood. For her father, that would have as much of a negative impact as if Janet had been seriously ill. She let him explain.

'Her daughter Pippa and her husband look like they're staying in the UK. Pippa's pregnant and is having a difficult time of it. Janet's going over to help.'

'So she's coming back?'

Sophie couldn't really understand her father's concern. Janet had taken several months' leave to help her daughter with her first baby, and that had been before Sophie had started working with the practice.

'That's the thing, darling. She isn't. She has registration in England and a job. Richard has some contacts, and of course they'll have no problems with visas.'

'Are they going soon?'

Ross Carmichael ignored her question. Something he often did when he wasn't happy with the direction of the conversation.

'So you must see, Sophie, I need you back home as soon as possible. This little *jaunt* of yours… If you're worried about what people think about that fiasco with Jeremy—'

'No, Dad. I'm over that. I just want to get on with my life.'

'Of course you do. I understand. So as soon as we can get you home… I can talk to this Dr Brent if you want me to. I'm sure we can work something out.'

At that moment Sophie realised how much control her father had had over her life, for longer than she wanted to admit. Well, she'd tasted freedom now. If she wanted to stay in Western Australia, if she wanted to continue working with Will for a week, a month or a year, it was going to be *her* decision. She needed time to think. She might well decide to return to Sydney when the eight weeks was up, but she wasn't going to be bullied by her father. She was determined to make up her own mind.

'No, Dad, I'm staying.'

'What did you say, Sophie? I must have misheard.'

'I'm staying. I've agreed to at least until the end of the month, and I'll let you know my plans from then on.' Her father was strangely silent. She took a deep breath. 'So I suggest you advertise for a replacement for Janet as soon as you can.'

'But, Sophie, you can't—'

'Yes, I can.'

And then Sophie did something she'd never done before. She hung up…before her father had finished what he'd wanted to say. She'd actually had the last word.

It felt good.

* * *

The next day, when Sophie arrived at work, she could hear animated chatter followed by muffled laughter coming from the tea room and was curious to know what was going on.

'What's the joke?'

Lisa and Sandie fell silent and exchanged looks, suggesting they might not want to share the reason for their amusement.

Sophie smiled. 'Should my ears be burning?'

Sandie stirred milk into the drink she'd made and cleared her throat. 'No need to worry. We're not talking about you, and you'll find out soon enough, so we might as well tell you.' Again she looked at Lisa and the nurse nodded.

'Go on,' Lisa said.

'It's the boss.'

'The boss?' Sophie was intrigued.

'We think he's had some kind of life-changing experience on the weekend. It took a double-take to recognise him when he breezed into Reception this morning.'

Sophie suddenly realised what they were talking about. She prayed that the increase in her heart rate and the sudden rush of whole-body warmth wouldn't give her away. Lisa didn't seem to notice as she continued where the receptionist had left off.

'He's bought some new clothes that are actually *trendy*—not mass-produced department-store stuff.'

'And had a haircut,' Sandie added with a grin. 'He looks absolutely gorgeous. If I wasn't a happily married woman...'

Both women fixed their gaze on Sophie. It took all she had to maintain her composure. Did they know?

'We thought he'd either won the Lotto or... We wondered if *you* might have had something to do with it,' Lisa said slowly.

'Me?' Sophie laughed and raised both hands to her shoulders, palms outwards. 'Why would what Dr Brent wears have anything to do with me?'

Sophie didn't want to hear the answer, and thankfully the conversation was interrupted by Caitlyn.

'It's getting busy at the front desk.' The girl was addressing

Sandie. 'And the phone's going non-stop. I could do with a hand.'

The women's attention shifted.

'Sorry, Caitlyn. I'll be right there.'

'Thanks. And you've got three patients waiting already, Dr Carmichael,' Caitlyn added, before she did an about-turn and hurried back towards Reception, with Lisa and Sandie not far behind.

Sophie took a deep breath, trying to pretend Saturday night hadn't happened. The logical part of her brain told her that if Will took the relatively small step of reclaiming some of his time for a social life he would find the perfect woman. He already had his female staff drooling and they were only the tip of the iceberg. It was just a matter of time.

The trouble was, her heart was sending her a completely different message. She wanted him for herself.

Sophie's day sped by with no time to stop and talk to Will, let alone admire his revamped appearance. Every time their paths crossed he was civil but economical with words. It was difficult to know what he was thinking. She was over the halfway mark in her stay and had begun to seriously think about the possibility of staying on.

The hints from Will about how he felt hadn't happened, so she was still undecided.

From her first day she'd found the work and the people she treated in Prevely Springs a challenge. The rewards weren't measured in terms of money and prestige, though, but they were certainly there for the taking if you were prepared to give that little bit extra. Job satisfaction was in a different league from the humdrum routine of treating the wealthy, who were often unnecessarily preoccupied with their own health, back home.

Home?

Did she really want Sydney to be home...for the rest of her life? She was beginning to have serious doubts now she'd experienced a way of life so different, so unpredictable, so interesting...and so full of possibilities.

After her father's phone call the previous day she'd felt angry and annoyed. He'd automatically assumed she'd do as he wanted and run back to Sydney because he *needed* her. He took absolutely no account of *her* needs and, in retrospect, he probably never had. All the important decisions directing the course of her life had been his. Medicine, general practice, Jeremy...

Maybe it was time to start taking control. Extending her stay with Will Brent could be the first step, but she still had a few weeks to make up her mind.

She tidied her desk, gathered her things and walked the short length of corridor to Will's room. His door was open and he sat at his desk, tapping away at his computer keyboard. He looked up when she knocked.

'Finished consulting for the day?' she asked.

'Just about.'

'Are you calling in to see Bella Farris tonight?'

'I am. I wasn't sure whether you wanted to come or not.'

'Do you mind if I do?'

'Of course not. I'll be ready to go in ten minutes.'

A short time later they set off in Will's car.

'Shelley phoned this morning and warned me that Bella's deteriorated. She suggested we contact her daughter.'

Will glanced across at Sophie, probably to gauge whether she understood the full implications. Although Sophie had only seen the Farris family twice, she felt she'd made an impression on Bella's withdrawn son. His mother's death would be an enormous stress for him but her training hadn't prepared Sophie for the reality of dealing with a fourteen-year-old's grief.

Her instincts told her she might add to his distress by deserting him. Brad and Bella Farris were two more reasons for her to stay on.

'She's in the last stages?' Sophie asked, choking back emotion she'd thought she'd be able to control.

'That's right.'

They made the rest of the short trip to Bella's house without speaking. When they arrived Brad was outside, manoeuvring a battered skateboard down the slope of the drive. He smashed into the letterbox and then repeated exactly the same sequence, the second time flattening the post. He seemed oblivious to their presence and the damage he was doing.

'He's angry,' Will said quietly.

'At his mother?'

'That's right, and probably at himself for what he sees as his helplessness; at me for not being able to provide a cure; at life in general for dealing him such a cruel hand. We'll have to tread softly with Brad over the next week or two.'

'You think that's all the time Bella has left?'

'I can't say until I see her, but from what Shelley said—'

Will's sentence was cut short by the thumping sound of Brad skidding past the car and apparently stopping by turning sharply into the back of the wagon.

'He's an accident waiting to happen. Let's get him inside.'

Sophie climbed out of the car while Will gathered his bag.

'You've been practising. I reckon that gives you an unfair advantage,' she said to Brad as he scooted past.

The last time Sophie had seen Brad he'd told her he planned to borrow a skateboarding game from a mate—an oldie but a goodie, he'd said, and had seemed keen to share it with her. She figured relating to the introverted teenager on any level was better than nothing.

Brad picked up his board and walked towards the house. Despite his distant expression, Sophie noticed the slightest smile. He left the front door open and when Sophie and Will stepped inside he was already setting up the games console. Will nodded in the direction of the boy.

'You don't have to come with me to see Bella.' He winked and whispered, 'I think you might have more important work to do with Brad.'

Sophie responded to his cue, walked across and sat beside Brad.

'I hope you've got the skateboarding game?' she said cautiously, trying to gauge the boy's mood.

'Yeah.'

He turned on the TV and loaded the game. The screen lit up with graphics and colours reminiscent of the 1980s.

'How old is this game?'

'Vintage.'

'Love the intro music.'

Some of the catchy digital sequences sounded vaguely familiar to Sophie, and dated the game as ancient, but Brad didn't seem to mind. The relatively simple game was no doubt for Sophie's benefit.

'You're seriously weird,' Brad said.

She'd obviously caught his attention by mentioning the music. He looked at her and grinned, and she took his comment as a compliment.

'I'll show you the moves,' Brad generously offered. 'There's a load of different courses. Do you wanna start with a race or ramp event?'

'A race, of course.'

Brad laughed as he selected 'Downhill Chase' and wasted no time in setting up the beginning of a two-dimensional urban obstacle course.

'I'll do a demo and then you can have a go on your own.'

The conversation they were having involved the longest strings of words Brad had uttered in the time Sophie had known him. It was a positive step.

'And then we race and see who's the better man,' Sophie said.

The next ten minutes Sophie spent crashing into fire hydrants, falling off ledges and causing traffic accidents—many times over and in no particular order. Brad, of course, reached four-figure scores and was merciless in making no allowances for Sophie's inexperience and lack of skill.

'I think I've had enough,' she finally said when her skateboarding alter ego ended up in an underground sewer. 'But you carry on.'

As Brad finished the course with his highest score yet, Sophie wondered how his enthusiasm and skill in electronic gaming could be transformed into more productive pursuits. He needed something in his life that would allow him to move forward after his mother died. He'd already alluded to not hitting it off with his sister's husband, but there was no alternative to him moving to Karratha when the time came.

What was he good at?

'You're way too good for me,' she said as Brad went to replace the cartridge with a single-player game.

'Nah, you're all right.'

Another compliment. Sophie was getting the hang of the understated language only teenagers understood. She laughed.

'No, I'm not. I'm hopeless.'

The noise of the new game began.

'You any good with computers?' She wasn't sure where her tentative question would lead.

'Okay, I s'pose,' he said, without looking away from the screen. It was as if he needed the buffer of the game to lessen the stress of a face-to-face conversation.

'Do you do computer studies at school?'

'Used to.'

'Why did you stop?'

'No point.'

'What do you mean?'

He stopped the game momentarily and looked at Sophie as if the question was out of line.

'I haven't got a computer at home. Most of the other kids in the class have.'

He concentrated his attention back on the game, signalling

the conversation was over, and Sophie knew it would achieve little to try and pursue the subject of computers further.

'I might go up and say hello to your mum, then.'

Sophie had gone as far as she could with Brad that afternoon. She also knew the time she had to help the boy was limited.

The change in Bella was dramatic. When Will had called in a few days ago she'd been holding on and he'd estimated her life expectancy to be in months. But now…

Her morphine dose had increased steadily. From the nurse's daily notes Will gleaned she was eating very little and was becoming weaker as each day passed. It was an effort for her to keep her eyes open.

'I'll organise oxygen for you, Bella, and see you as often as I can. Every day, if possible. Are you in pain?'

She opened her eyes. 'Nothing I can't handle.' Her husky voice was barely a whisper.

'I think we should contact Gemma.'

'Yes, Gemma needs to be here. It's not fair on Brad.'

Will saw a different type of pain in Bella's eyes. It was a kind of grieving pain. For the loss of time she wanted to spend with her son.

'Do you want me to ring her?'

'Yes. Thank you.'

'Okay.' He grasped the woman's cool hand. 'Shelley or one of the other palliative care nurses will continue coming twice a day and I'll see you tomorrow evening. By that time we should know when Gemma can come to help out.'

She nodded, exhausted by the effort of being examined and having to carry on a conversation.

Will gathered his things and turned to leave. He was surprised to see Sophie standing in the doorway.

'Have you been here long?' he said quietly.

They moved into the passage.

'Long enough.'

He thought he could see moisture in her eyes. She definitely wore her heart on her sleeve.

'Are you all right?' Will asked.

'Yes, I'm fine.'

He paused, but didn't want to press the matter.

'And Brad?'

'It's hard to tell. We didn't talk much but I think he's slowly coming out of his shell.'

'Good. Maybe we can talk about it in the car.'

They made their way down the stairs and said goodbye to Brad. Will hoped Sophie was making some progress with him because his own attempts had been unsuccessful.

When they reached the car he opened the door for his companion and the thought entered his mind that had been plaguing him all day.

What could he possibly do to make her stay?

Sophie could tell by the brief discussion they'd had in the car on the way back to the clinic that Will had developed the kind of emotional attachment to Bella that the training manuals suggested should be avoided. Sadness for a dying patient on a certain level was acceptable, but Will's involvement went deeper. If he responded to all his patients going through similar ordeals with the same intensity, he was headed for emotional burn-out. The usual debriefing process in this type of situation involved talking things through with a trusted colleague. To her knowledge, Will had no one to fulfil that role. Sophie wished she could help but didn't know how, without appearing too pushy.

When he asked if she would mind working on her own on Wednesday afternoon while he took a couple of hours off, she was happy to co-operate. He definitely needed down-time from work, and what had come to be known as the Springs Footy Derby was occupying most of his valuable spare time. Sandie soon set her straight, though. She should have known Will needed more than a couple of hours to turn off from the job.

When she returned from a lunchtime home visit the receptionist confided that leaving her in charge of the clinic was an unprecedented occurrence.

'Dr Brent has very important business to attend to,' Sandie said mysteriously.

'Oh,' Sophie answered, not wanting to pry. Sandie would tell her if she thought it worthy of a few minutes' gossip time. Sophie had learned in the time she'd been working at the practice that you told Sandie nothing you didn't want to become common neighbourhood knowledge by the end of the day.

'Aren't you interested in what it is?'

An answer wasn't necessary as the receptionist decided to tell Sophie anyway.

'He's meeting with the IT company that produces our medical software. He's been saying it's needed an upgrade for ages. You've probably noticed it's always crashing and there's two new versions come out since the 3.5.' She finally took a breath. 'But apparently our hardware is too old to cope, so Dr Brent's getting prices to replace the lot.'

'What? He's thinking of getting new computers, monitors...?'

'Even printers.'

Sophie's interest was mildly aroused by Sandie's revelations and it set her thinking. When she visited Bella and Brad Farris the following day she had the germ of an idea, and after returning to the clinic she made a couple of phone calls. The responses were positive. Although she had no clue whether her plans would work, she felt it was worth a try and wanted to discuss the matter with Will.

She hadn't had the opportunity to broach the subject with him but decided she'd make the time.

Today. Thursday evening.

She'd been out on a late home visit, and was pleased to see Will's car still in the carport but the patient parking area empty when she got back. Hopefully he'd finished for the day and would be free to talk to her. She nearly collided with him as she opened the back door to the clinic.

'Hello, Sophie. I thought you'd gone home.'

'Hi, Will. I've just been out to see Jim Cooper.'

'Anything I should know about?'

'Dizzy spells. He's only a couple of days home from hospital after a heart attack and I think the starting dose of ACE inhibitor is too high. His systolic blood pressure's fallen to a hundred and he has symptoms typical of postural hypotension.'

'Did you reduce the dose of the new medication?'

'Yes, he agreed to come in and have Lisa check his BP every day over the next few days.'

'Good.'

Will looked as if he was in a hurry to leave, but Sophie wasn't going to be put off. The time she had to organise things was limited.

'Can I have a word about another matter?'

He looked at his watch. 'I was on my way to see Bella. Can it wait until tomorrow?'

Sophie smiled. 'I called in to see her and Brad at lunchtime. That's what I wanted to talk to you about. Her condition has picked up since Monday and we had a good chat. I asked if she felt she needed to see you as well… She said to tell you she's feeling better.'

Will looked relieved. 'Okay, but let's not stand in the doorway. How about a coffee?'

Will made the drinks and they both settled in the tea room.

'Fire away,' Will said after he'd taken a long sip of his coffee and visibly relaxed. 'What did you want to talk about?' he added, looking genuinely interested.

'Well, you know how I've been seeing Brad Farris?'

'And getting through to him, from what Bella and Shelley tell me. Amazing after only a couple of visits.' He paused as Sophie took a moment to absorb his praise. 'Sorry, I'm interrupting.'

'That's okay. It's good to know others are noticing his... change in attitude.'

She ran her finger around the rim of her cup, wondering if Will would think her suggestion forward—arrogant, even. She was probably basing her opinion on her father, who had always been resistant to any changes in his medical practice that hadn't been his idea. Will had nothing in common with Ross Carmichael other than a medical degree. Will waited attentively for her to continue.

'I wondered what you had planned for the old computers.'

'The old computers? Sandie's dealing with all that. I gather they're so outdated they're worth next to nothing. I think Sandie said something about donating them to a senior citizens' group.' He sipped coffee and ran his fingers through his hair. 'But I don't really understand what that has to do with Brad.'

'Well, I was talking to Bella about how Brad was performing at school and she said he was going really well until the full impact of her illness struck home.'

'I'm not surprised his work suffered.'

'He was good at maths, topped his class in computer studies and kept up with his other subjects. One of the brightest kids in his year.'

'And now?'

'He's barely scraping through, and not doing homework or handing in assignments. He's dropped out of computing, which was an elective for the kids in his year who needed more of a challenge.'

'What are you getting at?'

'He says there's no point. He hasn't even got a computer at home and he'll be moving north when...'

'Bella dies.'

'Yeah, there's no softer way to put it. He feels he'll be a second-class citizen, living with his sister and her young kids. He doesn't get on with his brother-in-law, who's made it quite clear he'll tolerate Brad only until he's old enough to go out to work.

I gather as soon as that happens he'll be out on the streets. So...I was wondering...'

'Y-e-s?' Will said the word slowly.

'If there was any chance of giving Brad one of the old computers?'

Will looked surprised but was smiling.

'I think that's a great idea,' he said. 'We'd need to clean the hard drive—'

'Which you'd have to do anyway, even if it was going to the tip. I talked with Howard.'

'Howard Lin?'

'Mmm, when he was checking out the rooms for the new cabling this morning. He said he'd be happy to clear the hard drives, as well as set up a recycled computer—no charge. And he could organise the loading of basic software for Brad as early as the middle of next week if they start the installation here tomorrow and work all weekend.'

'You told him about Brad?'

'Sort of. In general terms. I also told him we didn't have much time.'

Will leaned back in his chair and whistled. 'Well, well. You've been a busy lady, haven't you? And you think this will turn a corner for Brad?'

'I do—even though the sceptics might call it a long shot. I hope it will give him a sense of identity and put those skills he uses in his hours of gaming to some use. Bella says she's left provision for an allowance for him in her will.'

'You've talked wills with Bella?'

'She brought it up. It means he'd have enough spare cash to at least get an internet connection if his sister isn't already connected, but I'd have to see how Brad responds. I don't want him to abuse our goodwill.'

'So you haven't mentioned it to him?'

'Of course not. I needed to discuss it with you first.' *And I might not be here for much longer.* She didn't dare voice her thoughts.

Sophie caught her breath, seeing the subtle change in Will's expression, as if he'd read her mind. She'd put off the inevitable discussion of what she'd do at the end of her eight weeks' trial. The truth was she still wasn't a hundred per cent certain.

'That's fine by me.'

'What?'

For a moment Sophie thought he was talking about her leaving Prevely Springs.

'Go ahead. Set things up with Brad and the computer. After all, you may not have much time.'

CHAPTER TWELVE

THE next two weeks flew by at whirlwind speed, and Sophie could hardly believe the derby was actually happening...the following day. The committee had gathered for its final planning meeting and the atmosphere in the small room at the rear of Prevely Springs Medical Clinic was electric.

'I don't believe you've put Brianna Sanders in charge of one of the food stalls,' Will said as they worked their way through the checklist. They'd reached item five—catering.

'She wants to be a chef. She's truly passionate about cooking and I'm confident she can do it. She's a bright, responsible kid—'

'Who fell by the wayside and needed someone like you, Sophie, to bring her back from the brink,' Colleen said with a grin.

'Exactly,' Sophie replied. 'And of course her mum's going to be helping her for most of the day.' Sophie attempted a persuasive smile before continuing. 'Anyone have any problems with that?'

The group was silent.

'Next item—public address system,' Will said with authority.

It took a couple of hours to work their way through the complete list and at the end they all sat back with satisfied expressions on their weary faces. Apart from a health and safety issue with the construction of the catwalk for the fashion parade, and a last-minute change of supplier for the drinks stalls, the preparations had gone extremely well.

'There's just one last thing I need to mention that isn't on the list,' Sophie said.

'And what's that?'

'Bella Farris.'

Everyone knew and in some small way had touched the life of the gravely ill woman. A mood of sadness descended.

'You all know she's determined to come tomorrow?' Several people nodded and waited for Sophie to continue. 'We've put everything in place we can think of to make it as easy as is humanly possible. Will's arranged transport by ambulance, and Shelley will escort her into one of the executive boxes on a gurney, hooked up to oxygen.' Sophie paused and took a deep breath. 'She wants to come for the last quarter of the match and I wondered...'

'Yes, go on.' Will's voice was husky with emotion.

'It was a last-minute idea and I ran it by both football clubs only this afternoon.' Sophie cleared her throat, giving herself a moment to hold back threatening tears. 'I wondered if you'd all agree to dedicate the match to Bella.'

There was a moment or two of feet shuffling and fumbling in bags for tissues before Sandie spoke.

'That's a wonderful...touching...generous suggestion, and I'm pretty sure I speak for everyone when I say, go for it Sophie.'

There were sounds of agreement, and Lisa got up from her seat to give Sophie a hug, followed by Colleen, and then Charlie reached across the table and vigorously shook her hand. Sophie had touched a nerve in the work-weary group who were teetering on the brink of the previous month's hard slog coming to fruition. It wasn't long before they were all standing, smiling, crying, hugging, congratulating and back-slapping.

Only Will stood back. Quiet and serious. Until the last member of the committee took their leave.

Then he finally spoke.

* * *

'I... I...'

Will wanted to say so much, but the words stuck fast in his throat. He felt the sting of unshed tears and the remorseless thumping of his heart.

He wanted to say so much...

'What's the matter?'

Sophie looked bewildered.

'Is it something I've said...something I've done?'

'It's everything about you, Sophie Carmichael.' A hundred clichés rolled through Will's mind, but it stuck on those three words that were always so hard to say. 'I... I...'

She had embraced with enthusiasm this rag-bag of a neighbourhood he called home; she'd breathed new life into a community that had seemed programmed to self-destruct; she'd touched so many hearts...including his; she'd unlocked a window in his tormented soul and let in the sunshine.

She'd turned his life around.

He loved her! Why was it so painful to tell her?

'I...just wanted to say thank you.'

'It was teamwork. You worked as hard as me,' she said without hesitation.

'But—'

Sophie took a step forward and spread her arms wide, ready to hug him. He needed no further encouragement. He wrapped his arms around her and felt the warmth of her body pressed against his chest. Her breathing synchronised with his as he gently stroked her shoulder, moving his fingertips to the bare skin at the base of her beautiful neck. She tensed, but as he continued the caress he felt her muscles relax.

'I don't know how I can ever thank you, Sophie,' he whispered, before placing his hungry lips on her forehead. She tilted her head to look in his eyes and invited him into the depths of her own.

'Just don't ever change, Will.' She tightened her grip around his waist and drew him even closer. 'You're one in a million.'

Sophie pulled away and reached around behind her back to release his grip.

They both stood, embarrassed and emotional, until Sophie finally spoke, putting an end to their intimacy.

'Big day tomorrow. We really should be going.'

'Yes, you're right. We should be going.'

Sophie sighed with relief as the final siren sounded and the capacity crowd erupted into a roar of cheering, whistling and raucous singing. The game had been close, with only two goals the difference, but in the end it didn't matter to Sophie which team won. The big winners of the day were the people of Prevely Springs.

The event had been a resounding success in more ways than one. The people, the lifeblood of the community they were trying to rescue, had turned out in force. Will had revealed to her he'd never, in the more than thirty years he'd lived and worked in the Springs, seen the community work together with such energy, motivation and optimism for the future—not only for themselves but for the next generation.

Sophie felt a hand on her shoulder and looked around to see a beaming Will standing behind her. They'd been too busy to spend much time together throughout the day, but during the little contact she had had with her boss she'd noticed a change in him.

He'd lost some of the intensity that had kept him on a narrow, joyless path of endless work and personal sacrifice. The frown he'd once worn like an identity badge had been, at least for the day, replaced by the generous, heart-melting smile he'd previously saved for rare special occasions. And the way he had treated her...

'We need to go down for the presentations,' he said quietly.

'Yes, of course.'

For the final fifteen minutes of the game Sophie had joined Bella, Brad, Gemma and Shelley in the glass-enclosed viewing box overlooking the ground. Bella had somehow summoned up the energy to cheer and clap when her beloved team hit the front in the last few minutes. She now looked exhausted, was battling to keep her eyes open, and welcomed the oxygen she'd initially rejected.

'I'll just say goodbye to Bella. It's been a huge thrill for her to be able to come today.'

Sophie touched Bella's arm and she opened her eyes.

'Hey, you two. Shouldn't you be somewhere else…sorting out the awards…making speeches?' She paused for breath and her angular face broke into a grin. 'I can't thank you enough.'

Will leaned forward and grasped her hand.

'There's no need. Think of how much giving you've done over the years. It's about time you got something back.'

The woman sighed, then glanced at Shelley, Brad and Gemma, who'd kept a watchful eye on her during the afternoon.

'Off you go,' she said. 'I'm in good hands.'

Bella pulled her hand from Will's grip and waved him and Sophie away.

'We'll call in and see you on Monday.'

As they left the happy foursome Will reached for Sophie's hand and intertwined his fingers in hers as he strode towards the exit. His grip was strong, assertive, and seemed somehow to exemplify the subtle change Sophie had noticed in him through the day. He seemed to be chipping away at the barriers that had unyieldingly prevented him from venturing into any sort of personal relationship.

The biggest change, though, was the transformation that had happened gradually over the past few weeks. He had begun to share the burden that had weighed him down for most of his life. A small chink had appeared in the armour he wore when anyone tried to get close to him. He was learning to trust, to confide and to share.

What a mysterious and complicated man he was.

And the more he revealed, the more Sophie loved him.

She loved him. There was no doubt in her mind.

But Sophie had no time to dwell on her thoughts as Will guided her up the steps to the catwalk—which had now been transformed into a dais—ready to take his place at the head of the queue of speechmakers.

Will was handed a microphone and he cleared his throat. The crowd stilled to near silence as he began to speak.

'Firstly I'd like to thank...'

He methodically worked his way through the long list of sponsors, donors and helpers. When he reached the end he took a deep breath and again stilled the crowd with his steady voice.

'And I also have an important announcement...' He swallowed and cleared his throat again before continuing in a strong, sure voice. 'You all know the match was dedicated to Bella Farris, one of the brave, quiet achievers of our community.' The silence continued. 'I have pleasure in announcing that this morning I received approval from the council to name the Prevely Springs soon-to-be-revamped sports ground—an integral part of the project we hope will breathe new life into the area...' He paused and smiled. Sophie held her breath in anticipation. 'The Bella Farris Recreation Reserve.'

Sophie glanced up and saw the look of surprise and pleasure on Bella's face.

That moment made all the blood, sweat and tears worthwhile.

The applause rolled in like a mighty wave and then subsided. Will hadn't finished.

'And I also want to acknowledge the driving force, the creative energy and the...' He looked at Sophie, his eyes full of tender gratitude. She was close to tears. 'The inspiration for us all to at least have a decent go at achieving what I thought was an impossible goal.'

He grinned.

'Dr Sophie Carmichael.'

* * *

Sophie sat in dappled shade in a corner of her small courtyard garden, reflecting on the events of the previous day. It was like a vivid, poignant dream. The takings from ticket sales, the fashion auction, food and drink had come to the amazing sum of one hundred and twenty-five thousand dollars. The final count on personal and business donations was expected to reach a cool hundred thousand at least. Even after costs, they'd reached their goal with money to spare.

Now she had to think of the future. In the frenzied build-up to the derby she'd hardly given the matter a second thought, but Will wanted her final decision…tomorrow.

She still hadn't made up her mind.

Her biggest problem was an agonising battle being played out between her head and her heart.

Her rational, objective mind told her to go home to Sydney. She'd had the break she needed to get over Jeremy. He was history. And although the experience of working in Prevely Springs had been positive, the only reason to stay on was if she was prepared to stay long term.

It wouldn't be fair on Will. He wanted a committed, long-term partner, and Sophie didn't fit the job description.

But her crazy, irrational, subjective heart was sending her completely different messages.

She'd fallen in love with Will Brent.

It was a scary realisation.

She couldn't ignore the strengthening feelings she had for her boss. She'd become accustomed to Will's daily presence in her life and she'd miss him if she left. More than she was willing to acknowledge.

She was undoubtedly attracted to him physically. But it was more than that. She yearned for him to enfold her in his arms; she craved to spend every moment of her days and nights with him; she was willing to share with him her deepest secrets. But even more alarming were her recurring fantasies of becoming his wife and soul-mate, having his babies and growing old with him…in Prevely Springs.

She was beginning to feel at home.

But their different upbringings and life experiences put them worlds apart. She was willing to work on those issues if Will was prepared to as well, but it wouldn't happen if she went back to Sydney.

She went inside, sat at the tiny kitchen table and opened her laptop. When she'd finished the letter she'd written to Will to formalise her intention to continue working at the Prevely Springs Medical Clinic she placed it in her bag, ready to give to him first thing Monday morning.

CHAPTER THIRTEEN

THE call came from Shelley just before lunchtime. Fortunately Will was between patients and only had a couple waiting that he hoped could be rebooked.

'Bella's asking for you,' she said simply to Will, and then lowered her voice. 'She wants to say goodbye.'

Will swallowed hard.

'I'll be there in fifteen minutes,' he promised.

He quickly logged off the computer, collected his medical bag and hurried towards Reception.

'I'm off to see Bella and I need you to somehow rearrange my bookings. I want the whole afternoon free. If you could ask Sophie—'

'Don't worry. I'll sort it all out.' She paused. 'And if you're a bit late tomorrow—'

He knew where she was coming from. She'd worked with him long enough to know that with some of his patients it was difficult to maintain professional distance. Bella was one of them. But whatever happened, he saw no reason why it wouldn't be business as usual the following day.

'It should be fine. Just leave things as they are for now,' he said.

When he arrived at the Farris house Shelley opened the door. 'Gemma's upstairs with Bella, but Brad's shut himself in his room. I'm not sure what to do to help,' she said from the doorway.

Will walked into the house with the nurse.

'How's Bella?' he said, knowing the news wasn't good.

'She's lapsing in and out of consciousness but quite lucid when she's awake.'

'Has she asked to see Brad?'

'No. She just asked for you.'

'Okay, I'll go up and see Bella and then I'll try and talk to Brad.'

When Will entered Bella's room it took him a few moments to focus in the gloom. The curtains had been drawn but he saw Gemma, close to tears, sitting next to her mother, holding her hand. On the bedside table sat a large vase of brightly coloured gerberas—Bella's favourite flowers.

'Hello,' he whispered. 'Is your mother awake?'

Bella's eyes slowly opened and she smiled.

'Thanks for coming.' She sighed and then took a deep breath. 'I have something…important to say…to you.' She closed her eyes briefly and then opened them again.

'It must be important,' he said.

She ignored his comment and gathered her energy. He waited.

'Dr Carmichael…'

'Yes? You want to tell me something about Sophie?'

'Shh.' Bella put her finger to her lips and continued. 'She's sweet…on you.'

Will couldn't help a smile and was rewarded by the brief twinkle in Bella's eyes.

'She told you that?'

'No, not exactly…but you don't have to…be a mind-reader…'

'You're wrong.'

'You're telling a dying woman…she's wrong? Humour me… Dr Brent…and don't let her slip out…of your grasp.'

She closed her eyes again and this time didn't open them.

Will glanced at Gemma, whose previously suppressed tears now trickled down her cheeks.

'She's a matchmaker from way back and I've never known her to get it wrong.' The young woman blew her nose and then sighed. 'Is there anything else we can do for Mum?'

'Just be there for her,' he said quietly, and then added in his thoughts as a fuzzy image of *his* mother flashed into his mind. *And love her.*

'Thank you, Dr Brent,' Gemma whispered as she stood to give him a hug. 'Mum's had nothing but praise for the way you and Shelley and the other nurses have cared for her.' A smile emerged from the tears. 'And the derby was one of the high points of her life. She hasn't made a big deal about it, but the match, the dedication, naming the sports complex... She was really chuffed.'

Will stood in silence for a few moments, not knowing what to say. 'You should be thanking Sophie,' he finally said. 'She did most of the work.'

Gemma gave his hand a squeeze before she sat down again. 'Can you let her know how grateful we are?'

'Yes, of course.'

Gemma wiped her eyes and sniffed.

'Shelley said she'd stay, but there's no need—'

'I can't do anything more for your mother but I'd like to stay. Not only for Bella but for you...and Brad.'

Gemma's tears began to flow again and she nodded.

'I realise she's not got long, and Mum would like that, I'm sure. To have the people she cares about by her side.' Her voice trailed off. 'If only we could get through to Brad.'

'Let me try,' Will offered.

'Thanks.'

Gemma's attention returned to her mother, whose pattern of breathing had changed. Bella's hands began to twitch. Will slipped quietly out of the room and made his way along the short passage to Brad's room. The door was closed. Will knocked softly.

'It's Dr Brent.' Will waited a minute before adding, 'Can I come in?'

There was no reply, but when he tried the handle the door opened without resistance. Brad huddled in the corner of his room where the computer was set up on a small table next to his desk. Will sat on the bed.

'How's it going, Brad?' Will intentionally left the question open, so Brad could choose the direction of the conversation.

The boy closed down the screen. Brad turned to face him.

'Okay, I guess.'

'The computer?'

'Cool.'

'Did Howard set it up with some decent software?'

'Yeah. It's not the latest version but it's all I need. He set up an e-mail account. And it's got word processing and stuff so I can use it for school. He said we could look at an internet connection when I move.'

'To Karratha?'

Brad's expression changed. He sighed.

'Yeah.'

'Not looking forward to it?'

Brad's silence said it all.

'You'll miss your mum.'

Brad turned away. He was crying, so Will waited a minute before he moved across and put his arm around the boy's shoulders.

'She loves you very much, you know, and if she had any power to change things she would. She's done the best she can.'

'I know,' he whispered as he sniffed and wiped tears away with his sleeve.

'Maybe you could go in and see her?'

'Maybe,' he said as he turned back to the computer and loaded a game.

It was Brad's way of telling him he wanted to be on his own, and Will certainly didn't want to force him out of his comfort zone. He had the feeling Brad would see his mother before the afternoon was out.

'I'll be downstairs with Shelley if you need me,' Will said as he softly closed the door.

Bella passed away peacefully two and a half hours later. Both Brad and Gemma were with her, and it was as if, content that she had tied up the loose ends in her life, she was free to leave.

Will stayed on to make sure Gemma and Brad were okay, as well as performing the medical tasks that had to be done. It was late afternoon before he finally left. He phoned Sandie to let her know his patient had died and that he was going straight home.

'If you need me for anything, don't hesitate to phone,' he said with a calmness he didn't feel.

'We won't need you!' Sandie stated with her usual assertiveness. 'Sophie's managing perfectly well with the few extra patients we couldn't reschedule. Go home. Forget about work for the rest of the day and relax. You deserve it.'

But taking her advice was easier said than done.

When he got home he felt physically and emotionally exhausted but he couldn't relax.

He kept thinking of Brad. Orphaned and bundled off to live with his sister and her family at a time when his loss would be causing him most pain. Will had no doubt that Gemma loved her brother. She would probably manage to provide for his physical needs but she could never replace Bella.

Will knew that first hand.

Although Will's grandparents had assured him his mother, in her own way, had loved him, he'd never fully forgiven her for abandoning him and then dying before he'd had a chance to find out for himself.

Brad would need the strength of Superman to survive the

future—*the great unknown future*. He hoped with all his heart that the boy would find the staying power to make his way in the world without succumbing to the kind of mistakes he himself had made in his youth.

To add to his worries, Will also had recurring troubling thoughts of Sophie.

Bella had been at least half-right with her home-grown wisdom. Although he doubted Sophie was 'sweet on him', as Bella had put it, he wished—perhaps naively—there was some way of ensuring she stayed in WA so he could at least find out whether his deepening feelings for her were reciprocated. Today she was supposed to let him know if her intention was to continue working at Prevely Springs or to leave.

Not knowing added to his restlessness.

Will turned on the TV to try and take his mind off ruminations that were making him more uptight, but early-evening television wasn't the solution. He selected a CD from the 1980s that, if he played it loudly and immersed himself in the dark lyrics, could help him forget today's problems.

After cranking the volume up to a level just short of annoying the neighbours, he went into the kitchen to see what he had to make a snack.

Standing in front of the open fridge, he stared at the bottle of wine and six-pack of beer he kept for the visitors he rarely had; thankfully he'd never been tempted to have a drink. His resistance to temptation was a sign of his strength of character. After his disastrous experience with alcohol abuse when he'd been a student, he'd pledged to never drink it again.

But tonight he felt edgy.

He felt dangerously close to breaking his pledge.

And he knew what he had to do.

Although Sophie finished late, and was feeling the strain of a long day, she wanted to see Will.

Sandie had told her of Bella's death that afternoon and she

guessed Will would take it pretty hard. If he didn't want to talk about it then that was okay—at least she would have offered. She also wanted to know how Brad was doing.

She'd also not had the opportunity to let him know she'd decided to stay on, and she particularly wanted to give him the news personally. If he was feeling down, maybe her decision might cheer him up.

As she drove into his street she remembered the first time she'd visited his home. She recalled his gentlemanly hospitality, the way he'd shrugged off her enquiries about his upbringing and his comforting hug when she'd revealed a painful secret from her past. The hug turning into a wonderfully sensual kiss should have alerted her to the possibility she might fall in love with the man.

And she had...tumbled head over heels in love with Dr Will Brent. She realised it hadn't happened overnight. It had crept up on her like the subtle arrival of warm, life-giving sunshine after a cold, desolate winter and now she couldn't imagine the loneliness of life without him.

She pulled up in front of his house and saw lights on. As she walked up the front path she heard muffled sounds of an old rock band, and when she knocked on the front door she wasn't surprised there was no answer as the music originating from somewhere in the depths of the building was loud. Using music to numb emotions was something she could relate to, but she felt oddly apprehensive.

Should she tell Will how she felt about him, and risk a knock-back? Could she cope with another humiliating rejection? Jeremy's heartless behaviour still stung.

Nothing ventured, nothing gained...

As she headed along the narrow side pathway to the back of the house the volume of the music increased and she quickened her step. Taking a deep breath, she rounded the corner. Bright lights shone through the curtainless expanse of glass dividing the kitchen-living area from the patio. She knocked loudly on the central door.

'Will, it's me,' she shouted, and waited a minute or two before peering through. It took a while before she located Will. He was sprawled on the sofa, his head on the armrest and his mouth slightly open. She could see the slow, steady movement of his chest as he took each breath. The remains of a sandwich sat on a plate on the coffee table and Will clutched an empty tumbler.

He looked peaceful and was sound asleep. Sophie smiled, deciding it wasn't fair to wake him. It was probably better to let him sleep off the stresses and strains of his day undisturbed.

Sophie wasn't sure what prompted her to scan the rest of the room before she turned to leave, and what she saw took the bottom out of her world. Her father's words echoed in her mind as the heaviness of disappointment descended from her heart to the pit of her stomach.

He was a drunk...had a problem with alcohol...an alcoholic...

At first she'd dismissed the spiteful words as being unsubstantiated malicious gossip. Then, when Will had opened his heart to her and told her about his drug abuse, she'd believed his addiction problems were in the past.

But now...

The evidence was there, before her eyes. A jumble of beer bottles stood empty on the kitchen bench and a wine bottle lay on its side on the draining board of the sink.

Even if he wasn't an alcoholic, he obviously still had a problem with binge-drinking in times of stress. A lethal combination.

Regardless of how strong her feelings were for Will, she couldn't even contemplate a relationship with a man who drank to excess, no matter what the reason. Alcohol and irresponsible driving had killed her best friend. It was a time in her life she would never forget...never forgive.

Her eyes brimmed with tears as she marched out of Will's

yard to her car. Her idyllic plans for the future disappeared down a deep, gloomy hole.

How had she managed to be blindfolded *again* to what stood blatantly before her eyes?

She fumbled with the remote and finally unlocked the car door, hunched behind the wheel and slammed the door shut. But she didn't start the engine. Her hands were shaking, her body felt drained of energy and her mind was a tumultuous riot of conflicting emotions. She needed time to pull herself together and reconcile what she'd seen with what she knew. She took several deep, tremulous breaths until she calmed down, until her mind was clear enough to look at the situation objectively. She couldn't have got it all so completely wrong.

Had her immediate, emotion-fuelled response been simply a spur-of-the-moment gut reaction?

Will wasn't a quitter.

Neither was he a drunk.

His strength, at times, seemed limitless, and it didn't make sense that he would find solace in alcohol. He'd been close to Bella but Sophie felt sure he could cope with her inevitable death. It was part of his daily work.

What her father had told her was based purely on hearsay. It didn't feel right and she had no reason to believe his gossip-mongering—especially when his motivation was surely to encourage her to go back to Sydney.

There must be another explanation.

Sophie gazed into the darkness, collecting her thoughts. *She loved Will*...and she was fast becoming hooked on a lifestyle and neighbourhood that, for the first time in her working life, was providing her with a gratifying sense of fulfilment. It was a good feeling. One she didn't want to relinquish.

And why should she?

The confusion in her mind suddenly cleared and she knew she had to talk to Will.

To find out the truth.

Tonight.

The noise tore into Will's sleep-addled brain like an angle grinder cutting through sheet metal. He opened his eyes and tried to concentrate. The high-pitched, intermittent sound was close but it wasn't music.

It was coming from outside.

A car horn blared…almost continuously…urgently.

What on earth was going on?

He strode barefoot to the front door, and when he opened it his reaction to what he saw was reflexive, almost primitive.

'Hey, what the hell do you think you're doing?' he shouted as he ran down the front steps and saw Sophie's car parked in the driveway.

Sophie's car?

Why was she parked in front of his house?

The two shadowy figures banging on the windscreen and shouting obscenities were suddenly silent, and then ran. Will thought he saw the glint of a knife in one of troublemaker's hands but he had no time to investigate—he had to see if Sophie was safe.

He thanked God her door was locked as he leaned over to peer through the window. Even in the gloom he could see her shrink back and that she was sobbing. She was terrified.

'It's me—Will,' he said calmly, with his face close to the glass.

'Will?' She fumbled for the controls and the window slid down. He heard the click of the central locking.

'They've gone and I doubt they'll come back.' He opened the door and her gasping sobs wrenched at his heart. 'Come inside,' he whispered. He had an overwhelming need to protect this fragile, frightened woman huddled in the dark.

She accepted his offered hand, and then suddenly she was

in his arms, clinging to his shirt as if her life depended on it. He embraced her and hugged her close until all her tears were spent.

'Come inside,' Will repeated as he steadied her stumbling gait and guided her towards the house.

He led her to the sofa and sat next to her. She began to shake again like a frightened animal. He enfolded her in his arms and held her close.

'What happened?' Will said gently. 'What are you doing here?'

Sophie turned, and her eyes—reddened from crying, pupils still wide and dark with fear—met his. She sniffed, cleared her throat and leaned slightly away from him. It seemed an eternity before she finally spoke.

'Bella...'

The worried expression on her face was edged with pain. He waited for her to continue.

'Sandie told me she passed away this afternoon and I just wondered...' She looked away. He wanted to soothe her, keep hold of her and never let her go.

'You wondered?'

'I thought you might want someone to talk to.'

Will's heart did an uncomfortable somersault. *She* was worried about *him*. In the guise of comforter she'd apparently landed herself in the midst of a terrifying altercation...on his front doorstep. Guilt burned in his gut. It had been a long time since anyone had cared about him that much...

They sat in silence for a few moments. Will felt Sophie's breathing steady and her heart rate slow. He reached for her hand.

'I'll call the police.'

The force with which she withdrew startled Will.

'No!' she said. 'They didn't hurt me or damage any property, and they were only kids—probably fourteen or fifteen. I panicked. I overreacted. There must be better ways to keep them off the streets.'

Now she was *defending* her attackers. It was difficult to comprehend how she could so easily forgive—after what they'd done.

'But they were—'

'No.' She reached for a handful of tissues and blew her nose. 'Forget about the louts.' Her gaze was now steady and her eyes dry. 'There's something else I want to talk to you about.'

It hadn't taken Sophie long, once she'd recovered from her distressing experience with the teenage hooligans, to realise Will wasn't drunk. His eyes were bright and brimming with concern, his movements steady and purposeful, and his breath smelled of herbs, piquant cheese and coffee.

She had no doubt in her mind that her tall, dark and handsome rescuer's head was clear.

She'd accepted his offer to make her a mug of tea and he was busy in the kitchen. It gave her a chance to collect her thoughts and work out what she was going to say. A few moments later he was back by her side and putting two steaming cups on the coffee table.

He smiled.

'What was it you wanted to talk to me about?'

Sophie paused to take a breath and wondered if she was doing the right thing, but she decided she needed to know.

'There's no easy way to say this. It's about…er…'

'Go on, I'm listening.' Will was frowning now.

'I know you don't drink, and I think I know why. My father—'

'Let me guess,' he interrupted. 'Your father has done some research and found a skeleton or two in your boss's closet.'

Sophie felt ashamed of her father's behaviour as much as reluctance to bring the problem out into the open with the man Ross Carmichael had accused of crimes he'd had no evidence for.

No secrets, she reminded herself. Honesty. She'd start right now.

'Something like that. He rang me a couple of times…' Sophie paused to take a deep breath. 'He told me he'd heard you'd had an alcohol problem when you were a med student.'

Will surprised her with laughter.

'And I bet he told you once an alcoholic, always an alcoholic, and to run a mile.' He brought the back of her hand up to his lips and kissed it tenderly. It somehow seemed the natural thing for him to do. 'That's in the past. I haven't touched a drink for nearly twenty years. And I don't intend to in the future either.'

'But…' The mess of empty bottles still littered his kitchen.

'But what?' Will said looking bewildered.

She clenched her hands in her lap. What she was about to tell him wasn't going to be easy.

'I was about to go home when those boys came out of nowhere.'

'Go home? I don't understand. Had you changed your mind?'

Sophie took a slow sip of her tea. She could feel the intensity of Will's gaze. He looked bewildered.

'I knocked at the front door. There was music but you didn't answer, so I went around the back.'

He smiled. 'I got carried away—sorry. Loud vintage music has the effect of numbing my brain when I get stressed—rarely fails to work.' His expression changed and she wondered if he'd suddenly realised what she'd seen. 'I've had one of those days.'

'But the bottles?'

'What bottles?'

'Over there on the sink. Wine and beer…empty…' Sophie's heart began to thud. She wondered if she'd just ended their embryonic relationship before it had had a chance to breathe fresh air. But Will was smiling again. He certainly didn't look like a guilty man.

'Ah, the bottles. It's confession time. They were empty because I tipped them down the sink.' He grasped her hand again, with a grip that indicated he wasn't about to let go. 'I keep a small amount of alcohol in the house for visitors.' He chuckled. 'Not that I have many. I pride myself in having the willpower not to touch it, and I haven't in twenty years. A couple of times I've come pretty close, and today was one of those occasions. So I tipped temptation away and I must have been sound asleep when you knocked.' He paused. 'Do you believe me?'

Sophie nodded. How could she not believe this open-faced, eager, gorgeous man?

'So your father was right. But it's definitely past history.'

Sophie smiled.

'I'm glad,' she said, and wondered how she could have not trusted him. There was nothing in this wonderful, giving man not to love.

'I love you, Will Brent.' The words came straight from her heart and spilled from her mouth before she had a chance to stop them.

Impulsively, she leaned across and kissed him on the mouth, and then sat back, startled at her own bravado. Will was silent. Stunned. Had she blown it?

'And I want to stay in Prevely Springs...if you'll have me.' It was a last-ditch attempt to get a reaction.

It worked.

He broke into a broad grin.

'Of course I'll have you, Dr Sophie.' His warm, soft lips found hers and he kissed her long and hard, with a passion that took Sophie's breath away. When he finally released her he sighed and whispered with a mischievous twinkle in his eye, 'But will you have me?'

She leaned across and rested both hands on his shoulders.

'Is that a business proposal?'

He laughed and encircled her delicate wrists with his firm, gentle hands. He kissed one palm and then the other.

'No, it's a marriage proposal.'

Sophie replied without hesitation.

'I will.'

EPILOGUE

A year later

SOPHIE stood in the newly refurbished kitchen of Brent's Place.
The building's official name was The Albert and June Brent
Community Centre, but long ago, when the rebuilding had only
just begun, the name had been abbreviated—and had tenaciously
stuck. It hadn't detracted from the elderly couple the centre was
dedicated to, though. Will had made sure of that. Over the past
twelve months, singing the praises of his grandparents had almost
become a mantra, and had been instrumental in bringing the
disparate community together to achieve their goal.

'Dr Brent, do you want these in the oven yet?'

Sophie still wasn't used to the title she shared with her husband of seven months, and it took a couple of moments before
she registered that Brianna Sanders was addressing *her* and not
Will. She was usually called simply 'Dr Sophie' by the adults
of the community, to save confusion.

She smiled at the sixteen-going-on-twenty-five-year-old who
was transforming into a confident and beautiful young woman.
Brianna no longer needed drugs to give her a high. She was
part way towards her goal of becoming a chef, and judging by
the wonderful food she'd helped prepare for the opening of the
centre Sophie had no doubt she would succeed.

'Stack the trays in the oven and we'll fire them up in about
half an hour.'

'Okay.'

After she'd loaded one half of the commercial-size double oven with a variety of savoury pastries, the tall, slim teenager peeped through the hatch, which provided a view of the gymnasium. For tonight's celebration it had been decorated with brightly painted posters provided by the year-eleven art class of the local high school and converted to a hall with seating for about a hundred.

'There are hardly any seats left,' Brianna said with a broad grin.

'I think nearly the whole of Prevely Springs is here.' Sophie beamed as well.

Will had cleverly involved a substantial number of the residents in the building and renovating process, which had not only provided a focus for many of the bored and unemployed young people but had also brought the generations together, with the older folk all too willing to share their knowledge and skills. And they'd come out in force for the official opening of the new facility.

Sophie scanned the room and saw many familiar faces.

'Is that Brad over there?' Brianna seemed to be doing a double-take.

'I think it is.' The boy had grown taller in the last year, lost some weight and had shed the veil of gloom he'd worn like a shield before his mother had died. Sophie and Will had seen him only a couple of months ago, when he'd first moved back to Perth. The boy had kept in touch, via regular e-mails, and had been over the moon when he'd been one of only two students from his school in remote Karratha who had won a maths and computer studies scholarship to one of the academically focused colleges in Perth. He'd been billeted by an elderly couple who lived near his college and seemed to exude new-found confidence, settling well into his new life.

'He's sure changed,' Brianna said, as her gaze lingered on Brad.

'Interested?'

Brianna laughed and gave Sophie a friendly punch in the arm.

'He's only just turned fifteen. I'm not that desperate.'

'No, I guess not. You can take your pick.'

At that moment she saw Will heading from the back of the hall towards the small stage where the Lord Mayor, several councillors and half a dozen of their benefactors, including Andrew Fletcher, were already seated. Will seemed to be looking for someone, and when he glanced in her direction he waved and beckoned her to join him.

'Looks like we're nearly ready to start and my services are required elsewhere.' She smiled at Brianna. 'Sure you can manage in here?'

'Of course I can,' she said, with a maturity beyond her years, and Sophie had full confidence in her abilities.

As Sophie joined her husband and they walked hand in hand down the central aisle to the stage, the audience began to clap and then burst into clamorous cheering. From the heat in Sophie's cheeks she could only imagine the colour of her face, but Will was beaming and apparently revelling in the noisy show of approval.

He gave her hand a squeeze and leaned close to her. If she wasn't mistaken, Will was close to tears.

'I wish Albie and June were here to see this.'

Sophie fixed her gaze on his and marvelled at how lucky she was to have found her soul-mate and life partner—in the most unlikely of places. She loved him so much.

'I think they're here in spirit, Will.'

He smiled. 'I think so too.' He paused at the steps on the edge of the stage and took a deep breath. 'And I have the feeling I can finally let go.'

Sophie knew at that moment that Will had fulfilled a self-imposed obligation that had been weighing him down for too long. He'd reached a turning point and she hoped he could finally move on.

As they climbed onto the stage together the audience stood as one and continued cheering, and Sophie felt a heady mixture of elation and pride.

She was home. In Prevely Springs. With the man she loved. Her free hand moved to the barely perceptible bump in her belly, instinctively protecting their tiny unborn child.

She smiled. They were a family.

What more could she possibly want?

JULY 2011
HARDBACK TITLES

ROMANCE

The Marriage Betrayal	Lynne Graham
The Ice Prince	Sandra Marton
Doukakis's Apprentice	Sarah Morgan
Surrender to the Past	Carole Mortimer
Heart of the Desert	Carol Marinelli
Reckless Night in Rio	Jennie Lucas
Her Impossible Boss	Cathy Williams
The Replacement Wife	Caitlin Crews
Dating and Other Dangers	Natalie Anderson
The S Before Ex	Mira Lyn Kelly
Her Outback Commander	Margaret Way
A Kiss to Seal the Deal	Nikki Logan
Baby on the Ranch	Susan Meier
The Army Ranger's Return	Soraya Lane
Girl in a Vintage Dress	Nicola Marsh
Rapunzel in New York	Nikki Logan
The Doctor & the Runaway Heiress	Marion Lennox
The Surgeon She Never Forgot	Melanie Milburne

HISTORICAL

Seduced by the Scoundrel	Louise Allen
Unmasking the Duke's Mistress	Margaret McPhee
To Catch a Husband…	Sarah Mallory
The Highlander's Redemption	Marguerite Kaye

MEDICAL™

The Playboy of Harley Street	Anne Fraser
Doctor on the Red Carpet	Anne Fraser
Just One Last Night…	Amy Andrews
Suddenly Single Sophie	Leonie Knight

MILLS BOON **JULY 2011**
LARGE PRINT TITLES

ROMANCE

A Stormy Spanish Summer — Penny Jordan
Taming the Last St Claire — Carole Mortimer
Not a Marrying Man — Miranda Lee
The Far Side of Paradise — Robyn Donald
The Baby Swap Miracle — Caroline Anderson
Expecting Royal Twins! — Melissa McClone
To Dance with a Prince — Cara Colter
Molly Cooper's Dream Date — Barbara Hannay

HISTORICAL

Lady Folbroke's Delicious Deception — Christine Merrill
Breaking the Governess's Rules — Michelle Styles
Her Dark and Dangerous Lord — Anne Herries
How To Marry a Rake — Deb Marlowe

MEDICAL™

Sheikh, Children's Doctor...Husband — Meredith Webber
Six-Week Marriage Miracle — Jessica Matthews
Rescued by the Dreamy Doc — Amy Andrews
Navy Officer to Family Man — Emily Forbes
St Piran's: Italian Surgeon, Forbidden Bride — Margaret McDonagh
The Baby Who Stole the Doctor's Heart — Dianne Drake

AUGUST 2011
HARDBACK TITLES

ROMANCE

Bride for Real	Lynne Graham
From Dirt to Diamonds	Julia James
The Thorn in His Side	Kim Lawrence
Fiancée for One Night	Trish Morey
The Untamed Argentinian	Susan Stephens
After the Greek Affair	Chantelle Shaw
The Highest Price to Pay	Maisey Yates
Under the Brazilian Sun	Catherine George
There's Something About a Rebel...	Anne Oliver
The Crown Affair	Lucy King
Australia's Maverick Millionaire	Margaret Way
Rescued by the Brooding Tycoon	Lucy Gordon
Not-So-Perfect Princess	Melissa McClone
The Heart of a Hero	Barbara Wallace
Swept Off Her Stilettos	Fiona Harper
Mr Right There All Along	Jackie Braun
The Tortured Rebel	Alison Roberts
Dating Dr Delicious	Laura Iding

HISTORICAL

Married to a Stranger	Louise Allen
A Dark and Brooding Gentleman	Margaret McPhee
Seducing Miss Lockwood	Helen Dickson
The Highlander's Return	Marguerite Kaye

MEDICAL™

The Doctor's Reason to Stay	Dianne Drake
Career Girl in the Country	Fiona Lowe
Wedding on the Baby Ward	Lucy Clark
Special Care Baby Miracle	Lucy Clark

AUGUST 2011
LARGE PRINT TITLES

ROMANCE

Jess's Promise	Lynne Graham
Not For Sale	Sandra Marton
After Their Vows	Michelle Reid
A Spanish Awakening	Kim Lawrence
In the Australian Billionaire's Arms	Margaret Way
Abby and the Bachelor Cop	Marion Lennox
Misty and the Single Dad	Marion Lennox
Daycare Mum to Wife	Jennie Adams

HISTORICAL

Miss in a Man's World	Anne Ashley
Captain Corcoran's Hoyden Bride	Annie Burrows
His Counterfeit Condesa	Joanna Fulford
Rebellious Rake, Innocent Governess	Elizabeth Beacon

MEDICAL™

Cedar Bluff's Most Eligible Bachelor	Laura Iding
Doctor: Diamond in the Rough	Lucy Clark
Becoming Dr Bellini's Bride	Joanna Neil
Midwife, Mother...Italian's Wife	Fiona McArthur
St Piran's: Daredevil, Doctor...Dad!	Anne Fraser
Single Dad's Triple Trouble	Fiona Lowe